Living with Flowers

LIVING
WITH
FLOWERS

Eszter Haraszty & Bruce D. Colen

LIVERIGHT NEW YORK

716

Library of Congress Cataloging in Publication Data
Haraszty, Eszter. / Living with flowers.
  Includes index.
    1. Flower arrangement. 2. Flower gardening.
3. Container gardening. I. Title.
SB449.H26 1980   635.9   79-29731
ISBN 0-87140-641-1

1 2 3 4 5 6 7 8 9 0

For B.D.C.

Who transplanted, thinned out, and weeded the words.

E.H.

Contents

Introduction

The dated pages and a small lock may be missing but, basically, I think of *Living with Flowers* as the diary of an infatuation; for, here, I have recorded a year's harvest of the flowers planted in my garden, the pleasures reaped.

It is a personal sort of diary in the sense that the flowers you will read about and see were all—down to the last weed—homegrown. While my garden happens to be in California, almost everything I grow can be raised in other sections of the United States, although the blooming periods are different. What are summer flowers for most gardeners across the nation—pansies, violas, pot marigolds, Iceland poppies, etc.—bloom in the winter out here.

There are other regional differences. Peonies, and two of my favorites, white lilacs and lily of the valley, cannot adapt to southern California's climate. On the other hand, easterners need the artificial atmosphere of a greenhouse to raise such West Coast regulars as mimosa, oleander, and hibiscus. Only with ideal weather and growing conditions can a weekend gardener in Connecticut hope to have marguerites half as large as those common to the

West Coast. However, beauty, color, and harmony—not profusion and size—are what make gardens and flower arrangements special. Besides, you never really know what will grow in a particular temperature zone until you try, and trying is a reward in itself when working with nature.

You do not have to be a landowner to color your life with flowers. As a former urbanite, I know the frustrations and expense of having to gather blossoms in a florist's shop. I hope that this book will encourage apartment and city dwellers to search out other sources. There are many alternatives and I have resorted to them all. Before moving to Los Angeles and the luxury of a first garden, I sustained my yearning for a house of flowers with blossoms that had been bought on a budget, gratefully accepted, begged, borrowed, or "appropriated." That last word brings me to the beginning of it all.

My father, a dedicated gardener, was never able to get me to help him around our country place, several hours outside Budapest. Planting, cultivating, weeding, and pruning were hardly competition for the carefree summer games children play. However, I would deign to climb down from the hayloft to assist when the gooseberries and red and white currants were juicy-ripe for picking. On the sly, I took out my wages in kind. Consequently, I was never asked to harvest the rarer, cultivated strawberries.

I loved picking flowers in those free and easy days. I gathered phlox, marigolds, and roses from my father's garden; Carpathian bellflowers and wild ferns in the woods; daisies, goldenrod, and black-eyed Susans along the roadside; and, in the fields of head-high wheat, I would gather the red poppies of Flanders and cornflowers. I still wander afar for floral bounty, although there has been a slight change in the ritual. As a child, once an armful of

flowers had been unloaded on my mother, the adventure was over.

Ironically, a war and twenty years later, when every second of my time was taken up becoming established in a new homeland, I was consumed by longing to be surrounded by flowers. Close friends with houses in Connecticut and Long Island knew of my yearning and called to say, "We desperately need a vacation from peaceful suburbia. Would you mind house and garden sitting for a few days?" Two close friends invited me to "Come on up for the weekend. The garden looks a mess and you can show us what to do about the weeds."

I returned from these missions with boxes of sickly plants—my diagnosis—which needed only repotting and fertilizer to bloom in my apartment. Conductors on the New Haven and Long Island railroads judged the coming of spring and the beginning of winter by my botanical luggage. The last armful of gold and crimson fall leaves meant they would not be seeing me for another six months, until the pussy willow and forsythia were ready to be forced. For everybody's sake, it was imperative that I start raising my own flowers. This was easier said than done on the asphalt fields of Manhattan, but I tried.

My studio apartment was the top floor of a brownstone on East Nineteenth Street, then called Block Beautiful, an oasis of lovely old houses, stoic trees, and courtyards. On the floor in front of each sunny window, I laid out apron-shaped gardens of potted plants and bulbs, resting in galvanized trays. When the ceiling in the studio area started leaking with each rain, I plugged it with a large skylight. Underneath, a four-inch-deep and very wide container held lily of the valley pips, planted at two-week intervals so that some would always be in bloom. After long days of fighting New York's depressing winter weather, that spot was a bright, sweet-smelling Welcome Home mat. Visitors to the guest bath could never gossip about there being a ring around the tub, for it was filled to the top with dirt. That tiny spare bathroom—the sunniest spot in the apartment, naturally—was my potting shed and nursery. I had converted the old-fashioned, claw-footed tub into an intensive care ward for the sick.

In window boxes, tulips shouldered their way through clusters of flowering geraniums, but seeing the former's shiny petals coated with soot each morning was dismal.

To my husband, Bruce Colen, a narcissus is someone who looks in the mirror a lot; and should I mention the word *aster,* he starts talking about the Airedale in the old *Thin Man* movies. When we met, the only flowers in his apartment were on the Kleenex box. One evening Bruce arrived at my apartment with a bouquet of snowdrops. The card tucked among the tiny flowers read: "Wouldn't it be lovelier to grow our own?"

We spent our honeymoon in Los Angeles looking for a home. I should say a piece of land—the house was incidental. Brokers quickly learned that we were more interested in fertile soil, good drainage, and sunny garden areas than closet space or the number of electrical outlets. We counted shade trees before bedrooms, sprinkler heads before baths. After our having inspected, and rejecting, some sixty-odd places, a persistent realtor telephoned to proclaim, "I've found it: nearly two acres of land, huge trees, lots of sun, a field of wildflowers. Even if you forget the house—and you'll want to, believe me—the place is a bargain."

We looked. We took. And, for a year, Bruce was convinced we had been taken.

It required that much time to partially remodel the structure into something vaguely resembling a house, to clear, cultivate, de-rock, de-gopher, fertilize, and plant the land. The former tenants had allowed the parched soil to go literally to seed: sage brush, chaparral, dandelion, and glove-defying thorny thistle. For nearly twelve months, we took nightly baths in Absorbine, Jr., picked thorns out of each other's hands, and culled burrs from our hair. But when the house was finally filled with the first harvest, the backaches and bills were bearable. I might have overdone that first glorious session of picking my own flowers and placing them throughout the house, for I recall Bruce saying: "It's a good thing we have a front door or people would never know if they were inside or out."

There were many excesses in those early years as a gardener. A wheelbarrow full of mistakes were made in the process of learning the best ways to raise and use cutting flowers. Patient nursery men and dirt-thumbed books on horticulture taught me most of the dos and don'ts. Nevertheless, it was only through personal experimenting that I was able to work out a system and style that reflected my feelings about how flowers should be handled once picked.

You shall see that I think of nature as The Master Flower Arranger. Follow her ways and you cannot go wrong. This book is an attempt to understand and copy some of her secrets. In that sense, I proudly stand guilty of plagiarism.

Eszter Haraszty

California
Summertime, 1979

Living with Flowers

From the Ground Up

Guests, wandering through our house for the first time, often exclaim that the pitchers and bowls full of flowers "go so well with the place." And they say it with surprise. But, blossoms and greenery are a natural reflection of one's personality. Arranging and using bouquets to dress your surroundings is one of the most satisfying, and probably the most overlooked, means of self-expression.

The flowers in our house look "at home" because my garden is planted with *only* the colors and shapes that we like and wish to live with. This way, when I take down a basket and shears to gather flowers for the house, I know I'll be happy with my selection. Not having sown any seeds of doubt, there is no need to stand over a particular blossom debating its merits as a cutting flower. I know the temptation, especially with your first garden, to plant two of these, a half dozen of those, and a seed packet of that because "maybe I'll like them." I never did and the odds are that you will not either.

The plant now, decide later, approach to flowers is similar to buying a painting for the living room you are not quite sure of,

Plant Only
What You
Like

thinking that it will grow on you in time. In two months, the picture is moved to a guest room. Unwanted flowers suffer a sadder fate. Either they are left, unpicked, to fade away in their beds or you take pity on the orphans and gather them up for inclusion in a flower arrangement. They ruin the bouquet, of course, since an element has been added that jars your taste. Aesthetic and emotional reasons aside, serious gardening is simply too hard a task to waste effort and time raising anything you are not completely enthusiastic about.

A big obstacle to being a discriminating gardener is the general reluctance to speak ill of nature's children. Some feel that it is almost as bad as saying you do not like the human kind. Nonsense. I am sure God seriously considers recalling some of his models, now and then. Artificiality in either kids or flowers is a bore. The waxy, showcase look of calla lilies, poinsettia, and bird-of-paradise particularly offends me, although I am sure they are pleasing to many other gardeners. Nor am I overly fond of spikey plants, gladiolas for instance. Canterbury bells, digitalis, and delphiniums are exceptions to the latter prejudice, probably because their blossoms are softer, less severe. Your likes and dislikes must prevail, if you are to have a style, a personality of your own.

The colors you use are an important part of that personality pattern. Color preference is probably the first aesthetic judgment a human makes. Before parents or teachers have a chance to inhibit, a child instinctively reaches for the brightest toy or crayon. This would seem to indicate that I am either in my second childhood or have never grown up, for warm, brilliant shades are still my favorites. They predominate in our garden and in the floral arrangements born there. The following chart is a color breakdown of the flowers I plant each year. You may wish to refer to it in planning your own garden or when hunting for a particular blossom to add a certain shade to a centerpiece or bouquet.

Charts are a quick and easy reference guide but they also can be deceptive in their simplicity. Categorizing flowers by color is a good example of the possible problems. There is a blossom to match every shade and hue in the rainbow. Furthermore, two different flowers, each called red, can be as different as black and white. It is important to understand this dissimilarity because each will contribute entirely different values when it comes to using them in flower arrangements. Take a Gypsy and a Mr. Lincoln rose. The former, being orange red, would fit perfectly in a bouquet of yellow, orange, and gold flowers, while the Mr. Lincoln has such deep blue, red tones, it should be used to accentuate flowers in shades of pink, lavender, purple, and magenta. Consequently, given these variables and having limited myself to only eleven color headings for the chart, the listings can only be approximate.

An equally insoluble problem is how to departmentalize multicolored flowers like parrot tulips and fuchsia. The faces on pansies and fingerprints have one thing in common—no two are alike. And to complicate matters further, each year growers bring out a tulip, an iris, or a rose in a new shade. In short, a chart of this nature can never be complete. However, it should be helpful for those who wish to plan a garden and future bouquets around colors that they prefer. When a flower comes in more than one shade, I have indicated the colors I prefer to raise with an asterisk. Variegated flowers are listed under their predominate color.

Having settled upon the flowers that please you most, plant them with a lavish hand, even if you seem to be violating an accepted practice. Gardening is a very personal activity and, as such,

And Plant Them Close Together

_____

From the Ground Up ⧽ 5

A PLANTING COLOR CHART

WARM COLORS

Yellow	Gold	Orange	Pink	Red	Magenta
acacia					
			anemone		
			anemone, Japanese		
			aster	aster	aster
			camellia	camellia*	
			Canterbury bells		
chrysanthemum, Korean			chrysanthemum, Korean	chrysanthemum, Korean*	
chrysanthemum, pompom					
			cineraria	cineraria	
			columbine	columbine (plus white)	
			cornflower		
cosmos*		cosmos*	cosmos		cosmos
			cyclamen	cyclamen*	
daffodil					
daisy, African*		daisy, African*	daisy, African	daisy, African	
	gloriosa daisy (gold to rust)				
			delphinium		
					digitalis
		firethorn*		firethorn*	
freesia			freesia		freesia
			fuchsia*	fuchsia* (plus white)	
				geranium (plus pink)	

Yellow	Gold	Orange	Pink	Red	Magenta
iris, bulb*					
iris, rhizome					
				Jerusalem cherry*	
		kalanchoe*		kalanchoe*	
			lily, rubrum* (*striped and spotted*)		
				lobelia	
marguerite*			marguerite		
marigold, African*		marigold, African*			
marigold, French* (*and yellow to rust*)		marigold, French*			
marigold, pot*		marigold, pot*			
narcissus*					
nasturtium*		nasturtium*		nasturtium*	
			oleander	oleander	
oxalis					
pansy*					
			petunia		
			phalaenopsis		
			phlox	phlox	
			pinks*	pinks*	
		poppy, California*			
poppy, Iceland*	poppy, Iceland*	poppy, Iceland*	poppy, Iceland*	poppy, Iceland*	poppy, Iceland*
primrose, English*	primrose*	primrose*	primrose*	primrose*	primrose*
			primrose, fairy	primrose, fairy	
rose*	rose*	rose*	rose*	rose*	rose*

Yellow	Gold	Orange	Pink	Red	Magenta
ranunculus*	ranunculus*	ranunculus*	ranunculus*	ranunculus*	ranunculus*
snapdragon*		snapdragon* (to red)	snapdragon		
squash					
sunflower*	sunflower*				
		sunflower, Mexican* (with red)			
			sweet pea	sweet pea	
tickseed					
tulip*		tulip*	tulip	tulip*	
			verbena	verbena*	
			wisteria		
zinnia*	zinnia*	zinnia*	zinnia*	zinnia*	zinnia*

COOL COLORS

White	Blue	Green	Lavender	Purple
allium				
anemone	anemone			
anemone, Japanese*				
			artichoke (and blue)	
				aster*
baby's breath				
		bells of Ireland		
bluebell of Scotland			bluebell of Scotland*	
camellia				
Canterbury bells*				Canterbury bells*
carrot				
chrysanthemum, Korean				

White	Blue	Green	Lavender	Purple
	cineraria*			
columbine*				columbine (*and white*)
	cornflower*			
cosmos				
cyclamen*				
daffodil*				
daisy, oxeye				
daisy, Shasta				
delphinium*	delphinium*		delphinium	
digitalis*				
eucalyptus (*cream color*)				
feverfew				
	forget-me-not, Chinese			
freesia*				
fuchsia*				fuchsia
geranium*				
iris, bulbs*	iris* (*and dark blue*)			iris*
iris, rhizome*	iris*			iris
lily, Goldband (*yellow stripes, pink spots*)				
lily, Regal (*and yellow with pink spots*)				
lily of the Nile*			lily of the Nile	
lobelia*	lobelia*			
marguerite*	marguerite			
marigold, African †				

White	Blue	Green	Lavender	Purple
	morning glory			
		moss, Scotch		
narcissus*				
			nightshade, Paraguayan	
oleander*				
pansy*	pansy*			
periwinkle				
petunia*	petunia			petunia*
phalaenopsis*				
phlox*	phlox			
poppy, California (*more cream than white*)				
poppy, Iceland*				
primrose*				
Queen Ann's lace*				
rose*			rose*	
ranunculus*				
snapdragon*				
snowball*				
sweet alyssum*				sweet alyssum
sweet pea*	sweet pea			sweet pea
tulip*				tulip
verbena	verbena			
				viola
wisteria*				wisteria
zinnia*		zinnia*		

†*Burpee recently developed this strain.*

you have every right to make your own house rules if they work—and your own mistakes, if they do not. For example, I use a great many annuals. There is the extra work of planting them anew each year, but they provide more of the colors I like. When the garden guides say to set them so many inches apart, I usually cut the distance almost in half. For, besides liking the look of flowers in massive clusters and disliking patches of nonproductive soil, I have found that they seem to thrive on close company. Also, weeds have difficulty getting started in such tight quarters. Finally, when plants grow so close to each other, their earth is shaded from the sun and dries out far less frequently, thus eliminating the constant cultivation of hard, crusted soil.

To avoid discrepancies between visualizing your ideal garden and the end result, outline the shape and size of proposed flower beds on a sheet of graph paper. Such a planting map can be very rough, since the primary purpose is to lay out your areas of color and to judge just how many bulbs, plants, or packages of seeds will be required to fill each bed. Indicate within the color patches the type or types of flowers you wish to use. With such a sketch in hand, and an estimate of the dimensions of your various flower plots, any nursery can fill your order accurately, reducing the chances of your overbuying or having to come back for more.

In Chapter 9, you will find the basic regional information for growing each of the blossoms that are shown in the photographs illustrating these words; but, since the book is primarily about the technique and pleasures of my kind of flower arrangements, I shall not get overly involved with the technical aspects of horticulture. There are too many fine gardening manuals and excellent magazines available for those in search of the how, when, and wheres of raising plants and bulbs. Nor should curious gardeners overlook the wealth of practical planting tips that are included in the mail-

Where to Go for Gardening Advice

order catalogues put out by some of the best seed, bulb, and plant firms: The Wayside Gardens Co., Hodges, South Carolina; W. Atlee Burpee Co., 300 Park Avenue, Warminster, Pa.; Geo. W. Park Seed Co., Inc., P.O. Box 31, Greenwood, South Carolina; Armstrong Nurseries, Inc., Ontario, Calif.; R. H. Shumway Seedsman, 628 Cedar Street, Rockford, Illinois. The most helpful and charmingly written brochure of them all comes from White Flower Farm, Litchfield, Conn. Called *The Garden Book*, it is published twice a year and, along with a complete botanical description of every bulb, seed, plant, and bush offered for sale, there is a thorough discussion of its planting needs. It is a truly valuable gardener's aid.

And, over the years, I have found that one good nursery owner is often worth more than all the manuals when it comes to solving regional gardening problems. On a personal level, they usually love what they sell and are anxious that your purchase does not die because of ignorance or neglect. As businessmen, they know that a successful, contented gardener will be a customer for life.

Of course, one of the most dependable and authoritative sources for gardening information are the agricultural extension departments of the various state universities. They will answer questions by mail or over the telephone; and some have the facilities and scientists to diagnose a particular disease when sent plant or earth samples. Many gardeners across the nation are lucky enough to have a county farm agent in their area to whom they may bring their problems. While these gentlemen work primarily with commercial farmers, they are experts on climate, soil conditions, and effective pesticides for their region.

The same sort of free advice can usually be obtained from local horticultural societies, gardening clubs, and botanical gardens.

The American Horticultural Society, Mount Vernon, Virginia, publishes a listing of all these groups. Finally, a wide assortment of instructional booklets are put out by the United States government. For a complete listing of pamphlets furnished by the Department of Agriculture, write: Superintendent of Documents, Government Printing Office, Washington, D.C. 20250, and ask for Bulletin #11, enclosing 45 cents.

Still, neither books nor experts can prescribe what sort of garden will work best for you. The layout of floral beds and what is going to rest in them are decisions that depend upon each individual's aesthetic approach and personal needs. By combining two elements, the visual and the practical, you eventually arrive at the most rewarding of all gardens: a functional one. Optimum beauty with minimum upkeep is every gardener's dream. I have not realized mine yet; but, after eighteen years of experimenting, I may be a little closer. In any event, I have learned a lot along the way.

One of the first discoveries was how much beauty and effort is wasted by thinking in terms of cutting gardens as distinct from display areas. Just as I desired a light, open house where one had the feeling that the floral world had been invited in as a permanent guest, when I stepped outside, I wanted the total impact of a giant flower arrangement of individual bouquets. That effect cannot be achieved if you grow tulips for the house behind a hedge or relegate daisies "for cutting" to a distant part of the property where the depleted bushes will not be noticed. Floral segregation is foolish and counterproductive. Every flower you grow should be for cutting; the trick is to have another in readiness to fill its place or camouflage the gap.

This would seem a good time to suggest that certain flowers look far better when cut and placed in an arrangement than they do

*Some Flowers,
More Than
Others, Are
Meant for
Cutting*

growing in the garden. Personally (and I can hear the roars of protest now), roses are a good example of such beneficial metamorphosis. Of course, some people can afford the time and upkeep to maintain a large and formal rose garden, containing dozens of different varieties. But with a few ungraceful bushes stationed here and there, the total harmony of a garden is disturbed. Even more important, only a rose isolated from its woody stem and dullish leaves can be fully appreciated. One magnificent blossom in a bud vase or a dozen white ones just opening in a simple pitcher are more inspiring, more beautiful, than a whole bed of bushes in bloom. I have a similar reaction to one of my favorites, the sunflower. Only if grown in mass, or when seen as lone pivoting sentinels in a farmer's hay field, do they lose their gangly, top-heavy look. Cut down to room size, all their awkwardness and imperfections vanish. Each summer, those massive golden heads stand in tall containers around our yellow living room, dripping pollen until puddles of sunshine form on the oak floor and tabletops.

*Camouflaging
to Disguise
Barren Areas
in a Garden*

I depend on a system of camouflaging to hide the gaps left by flowers that have been cut or finished blooming. For example, from the driveway to our front door, one passes beside a garden planted primarily in blues: forget-me-not, iris, pansies, violas, grape hyacinth, violets, bluebells, delphiniums, cornflowers, and ageratum. Bordering the entrance walk is a row of small, young daisy bushes. It is between the latter that our tulips, white and purple, put on their springtime show. Unfortunately, the performance is brief. Between the tulips cut for the house and those left to parade for a few weeks before their blue neighbors, the time soon comes when nothing is left but the decapitated plants. Nevertheless, the green basal leaves must stay put, if the bulbs are to regain their strength and bloom again the following year. This dying-off stage is hardly a visual treat but, just as the tulip season ends, the marguerites put on a burst of speed and cover the expiring plants with a throw of white blossoms. Now I know that daisy bushes will not time their blooming so propitiously for easterners, but every region has its perennials and/or evergreens to shroud the dearly departed. In the rose section of our garden, there are other rows of tulips, this time reds and yellows. One never notices when these die; for, by then, the rose bushes have hogged all attention with a waist-high offering of spectacular blooms.

Roses bloom from April to Christmas in California. That is too long a time for shading out the sunshine with another tier of green camouflage if I want any rose buds and blossoms for the house. A workable solution was to plant the bushes in front of a distracting backdrop. One end of a rabbit, bird, and deer-defying cage, which houses our vegetable garden, seemed the perfect spot. When that

wire wall is not covered with ten-foot-high white sweet pea, it is a trellis for tomato and cucumber plants. The rose bushes don't stand a chance of attracting much attention with such appetizing greenery looking over their shoulder.

There are so many different flowers and they come in so many different sizes that, one day, I sat down and made a list of the approximate heights of the ones I wished to grow (see chart). Also, the listing will give you some ideas as to what flowers are tall enough to mask the woody undergrowth of another plant or to cover bulbs and annuals that are dying off, etc. The heights are all predicated on a properly watered and fertilized garden. Naturally, with constant feeding and optimum temperature conditions, one can grow giants, but we are not after a new entry for the *Guinness Book of Records.*

While I do not have a formal garden in the symmetrical, blueprint-precise meaning of the phrase, it does not follow that the floral landscaping was done quixotically. In laying out the planting areas, I tried to balance appearance with practicality. My goal was a beautiful, satisfying garden, yet one that could be taken care of by a person with a strict, time-money budget. While I can think of no more lovely life than spending every day helping and watching plants grow, there are other things that must be attended to.

"Layering" to Save Work and Plants

From what better counselor than nature herself can we learn how to simplify botanical and human life? Take such a basic natural law as water-hungry flora sharing the same habitat. Follow suit in planting your beds, without being too visually obvious about it, and you'll save an hour or so a week dragging the hose from one part of the garden to another. Equally important, you will have created a small climatic world in which each inhabitant helps the other to prosper, from the tallest plant to the lowest ground cover.

PLANT HEIGHTS

Under One Foot

allium

aster
(*up to 2'*)

baby's tears

cyclamen

freesia

lobelia

marigold, dwarf

marigold, French

narcissus

oxalis, yellow

pansy

petunia
(*up to 3'*)

pinks
(*up to 1½'*)

poppy, California
(*up to 2'*)

primrose, English

primrose, fairy

rose, miniature

snapdragon,
miniature

sweet alyssum

sweet pea, dwarf

tulip
(*up to 2'*)

verbena
(*up to 1½'*)

Between One and Three Feet

anemone

anemone, Japanese (Alba)

baby's breath

bluebell of Scotland
(*up to 2'*)

Canterbury bells
(*up to 4'*)

chrysanthemum

chrysanthemum, pompon

cineraria

columbine

cornflower

daffodil

daisy, gloriosa

daisy, oxeye

daisy, Shasta
(*up to 4'*)

daisy, Transvaal

delphinium
(*up to 6'*)

feverfew

forget-me-not, Chinese

foxglove
(*up to 4'*)

fuchsia
(*up to 5'*)

geranium

iris, bearded
(*up to 4'*)

Over Three Feet

artichoke
(*up to 5'*)

camellia
(*up to 45'*)

cosmos
(*up to 10'*)

firethorn
(*up to 6'*)

lily, Goldband
(*up to 12'*)

lily, Regal
(*up to 6'*)

morning glory
(*10'–15'*)

nightshade, Paraguayan
(*up to 6'*)

oleander
(*up to 20'*)

Queen Ann's lace
(*up to 4'*)

rose, climbing
(*8'–20'*)

rose, grandiflora
(*5'–7'*)

rose, hybrid
(*up to 6'*)

rose, tree
(*4'–7'*)

snapdragon, giant

snowball, Japanese
(*up to 9'*)

Under One Foot	Between One and Three Feet	Over Three Feet
viola	iris, Japanese	sunflower (6'–10')
zinnia, buttons	Jerusalem cherry (up to 4')	sunflower, Mexican (up to 6')
zinnia, Lilliput	kalanchoe	wisteria
zinnia, Thumbelina	lily, rubrum	zinnia, California giants (up to 4')
	lily of the Nile	
	marguerite	
	marigold, African	
	marigold, French	
	marigold, pot	
	nasturtium (up to 4')	
	peppermint	
	periwinkle, Madagascar	
	phalaenopsis	
	phlox	
	poppy, Iceland	
	ranunculus	
	rose, floribunda	
	snapdragon, standard	
	sweet pea	
	tickseed	
	zinnia, cactus-flowered	
	zinnia, dahlia-flowered	
	zinnia, Zipasee, hybrid	

In short, by approximating nature's system of stratification, the weakest flora is protected by escalating levels of stronger and bigger plant life. I call the establishment of these all-for-one-and-one-for-all botanical societies "layering." Here is how it works.

In our dining area and the adjoining solarium are two ten-foot-wide, floor-to-ceiling windows, which look out on a terrace, surrounding gardens, and mountains in the distance. It is a very special view, but the expanse of cold glass needed softening. A see-through, living green curtain seemed right. So, we removed bricks from the terrace to make a semicircular planting bed in front of each window. Being on the north side of the house and under an overhanging roof, these were perfect places for plants and flowers that preferred a minimum of direct sunlight. However, the sun in southern California has a troublesome way of sticking its hot face where it is not wanted. I decided to layer those areas for shade.

We started with a mulberry tree in the center of each bed. They are very fast growers and a deciduous tree was chosen so no foliage would block the sun's milder, winter rays. Before we knew it, the original fifteen-gallon-size trees had large, leafy crowns fourteen feet in diameter, more than enough to shield the plantings to come and to spread their cool shade over the two skylights. Then, a staggered row of wire baskets lined with sphagnum moss and filled with asparagus fern was hung from the eaves. The third and fourth layers consist of ferns, the tree variety, and then, closer to the ground, smaller mother ferns and the like. The fifth level consists of gifts, planted by others: Jerusalem cherry bushes, sprouted from bird-strewn seeds; more asparagus fern, offsprings of those parents in the hanging baskets; and clumps of forget-me-not. The last were started there by "Christmas," our golden retriever, who smells a patch of the tiny flowers, gets the seed pods caught in her

Using Plants as a Sunshade for Flowers

coat, and wanders about the place, like Johnny Appleseed, tacking down a carpet of blue.

Next, a quilt of color is thrown over the bed: violets and cineraria. If I lived in Connecticut, my choice would probably be lily of the valley and members of the Vinca family. Finally, the lowest layer is a moisture-loving ground cover. I used baby's tears, but any member of the moss family or a specie of wandering Jew would be fine.

The end result: a seven-story condominium wherein all the tenants prefer shade and where the landlord saves on maintenance;

for, by the time you have thoroughly soaked the hanging baskets and sprayed the ferns, every other plant has received an adequate share of water.

I also discovered that one can layer for shade by actually *growing* umbrellas. A hundred-and-fifty-foot continuous line of marguerites had been planted to outline the northern perimeter of the garden-terrace area. Only when the whitecapped hedge had grown to full size, did I discover that daisy bushes cannot tolerate a whole summer of direct California sunshine. Some sort of cover for the border had to be devised or each year the marguerites that died of sunstroke would have to be replaced. The shade layer could not be anything as tall as a tree, or the wonderful north view of valley and mountains would be blocked. While wondering how to solve the problem, I recalled having read about the stylized trees that used to be fashioned from a lowly vine, a member of the potato family, called *Solanum rantonetti*. It has a small—about an inch across—lavender blue flower with five purple ribs and a tiny yellow and orange dot at the center. They also come in a white specie, but it is much harder to find these days, although back in the twenties and thirties the lighter ones were a favorite of Santa Barbara estate owners, who trimmed the *solanum* into bushy low trees to line driveways and garden walks. I decided to revive the practice, only I would train the vine into low, umbrella-shaped trees and station them at ten-foot intervals among the border marguerites.

Starting with a single *solanum* runner, which has been rooted and braced upright with a stick and twine, the vine takes about two years until it is chin high. During this training period, you must snip off any side-shoots so that all the strength is channeled into the crown of the sapling. In the third year there will be enough of a leafy top to warrant shaping with shears. Keep the *solanum* tied to

Growing Your Own Umbrellas

_____

From the Ground Up ≈ *21*

a heavy stake; for, the umbrella-formed tops react in a sudden gust of wind just like their silken counterparts.

Solanum will not survive in colder climes; but there are substitutes, say pyracantha (firethorn), forsythia, or tree roses, all of which can be similarly trained as living green umbrellas. I keep hoping that one day I will find the time to make a live parasol to shade our terrace table. It shouldn't be too hard a task, if I remove the canvas from a sturdy patio umbrella and train ivy up the pole and out on to the wire ribs.

Portable and Planter Bouquets

Inevitably, there are times when you are caught without a flower in the house: relatives suddenly drop by, or you meet some people at a cocktail party and over your third drink invite them home for an impromptu supper. Worse yet, you may spend so much time preparing a special dinner for friends that there is no time to put together a floral centerpiece worthy of the occasion. At these and other moments, it would be wonderful to have ready-made, live bouquets waiting in the wings.

It is possible. I call these ever-ready understudies Instant Flower Arrangements. I am talking here about pots and small tubs, filled with a variety of flowering plants and kept, most of the time, in a sunny spot close to the house, on an apartment terrace, or on the back porch or perhaps the front doorstep. Wherever they are stationed, these containers are meant to be brought indoors when you run short or out of cut flowers.

Even with a house full of blooms, we bring potted arrangements in from the terrace because, basically, there is really no substitute for cut flowers—except uncut ones. Potted bouquets live today to bloom and please another day. Staggering the height of the plants in portable arrangements produces a three-dimensional, pastoral quality. They give the impression that a square foot or two of nature has been dug up and set down in the house. To heighten this effect, I always place a few of the pots together on the floor in a corner of the room beside a sofa or on the hearth—when the fire is not lit. And as they look so bright and doubly alive in the company of greenery, I usually nestle several of the miniature gardens among the ferns and ivy in the solarium.

Containers Used for Camouflage

Ours cannot be the only house that has cracks and flaws that catch the eye: a section of floor tile in need of new grout, a corner of the baseboard that the dog once decided was a particularly tasty teething spot. I camouflage these imperfections so that guests see a tub of primroses and violas standing here, a large clay bowl of fuchsia and lobelia resting there, and the imperfections of the house are hidden.

If your guests are the sort who come for dinner and stay a week, the jig is up. Portable flower arrangements should not remain in heated, sunless rooms for more than two, perhaps three days. During their period of confinement, they must receive a daily, humidifying spray. Also, check the soil in *each* container (different plants have different drinking habits) to be sure that it has not dried out. I often think of these multiflower pots as being borrowed from nature like books at the public library. If returned on time, there is no penalty to pay.

The Variety of Portable Bouquets

The variety of flowers and colors in these live arrangements is as wide as individual taste, but you should keep in mind the indoor areas where they may be used. Each season I experiment with different combinations. This year's favorite for the living room is a four-layered affair in a terra-cotta bowl, four inches deep and fourteen inches in diameter. A single aster looks down on Chinese forget-me-nots and they, in turn, lord over two different breeds of marigolds, Nugget and Petite. For the bottom layer, and spilling out over the rim of the container, are lobelia and sweet alyssum. That may seem like a lot for such a small space but, actually, additional layers might have been worked in. The more the merrier. However, crowding plants together calls for extra horticultural attentions, which I will come to shortly.

Seeing how well those orange and yellow marigolds took to pot culture, I have decided to experiment next with a portable bouquet containing only marigolds. It is one of the few flower families I can think of that lends itself so well to the principle of layering. There are so many types and sizes. For example: the African marigolds grow to a height of three feet; the Crackerjack variety reaches two feet and First Lady a foot and a half. Nuggets are twelve inches

Primroses in wine goblet—Marigolds in carved duck.

tall, while the Petites range between six and eight inches. By looking through a few seed catalogues, you can find other varieties that
fit between these. There is an added advantage to using live, potted marigolds for floral displays. Once cut and placed in water, the
leaves of these plants rot very quickly. The resulting odor is not
one you would associate with a bouquet. Consequently, when you
use members of the marigold family as a cut flower, take off all
their foliage and employ some other kind of greenery—sometimes
I use celery tops from the vegetable garden.

It must be obvious that I am a staunch advocate of container
gardening as a convenient adjunct to cut flowers for the home.
The truth of the matter is, my enthusiasm goes much farther than
that. After spending eighteen years trying to keep one step ahead—
and falling one behind—of the myriad chores involved in maintaining and supporting an acre and a half in the fashion to which
we had made it accustomed, I often dream of another house, one
where my love of gardening could be pursued on a smaller scale. I
would still envelop our life with nature's gifts, but much, much
more of the planting would be done above ground. There would be
small courtyards and a large terrace filled with hanging baskets,
flowering trellises, raised beds, tubs and pots in every shape and
size. Even the stone and brick walls would be built so that they
supported flowers and greenery. I do not want a push-button
house, simply a garden that doesn't push me around.

The Advantage of Container Gardening

I have been slowly getting ready for that lovely day by practicing
with the fifty or so containers scattered about our present terrace,
two roughly circular brick areas connected by a rose-trellised
archway. All of the flower groupings may be seen from windows in
the kitchen, dining area, living room, solarium, and master bedroom, which is one more way of having nature as a house guest.

PAGE 26

Besides those ferns dangling beneath the mulberry trees, there are a dozen other hanging baskets, these filled with color: nasturtiums, geraniums, fuchsia, begonias—I continually marvel at the beauty of the tiny, strawberry begonias—pansies, petunias, Carpathian Bellflower, forget-me-not, lobelia, and even a few Jerusalem cherry bushes.

Turning a Terrace into a Garden

The various containers range in size from a six-inch clay pot holding Extra Dwarf zinnias to huge yellow daisy bushes in twenty-five-gallon wooden tubs. In between is an assortment of terra-cotta and earthenware planters. These have no fixed positions on the terrace. To the contrary, I periodically shuffle them about to produce a changing landscape and to satisfy their shade or light requirements. One of the wonderful things about gardening in movable containers is that by simply swiveling them a half turn you guarantee each plant having its place in the sun. Some of the smaller ones are grouped together to form pools of bright color on the weathered brick. If one of these pots is too low, or to achieve staggered elevations, I raise them with bricks, rather like slipping telephone books under a child until she reaches dinner-table level. Other containers rest on tables or atop plinths of pine and redwood logs.

In one place, we took up two square feet of brick to unfurl one of my *solanum* umbrellas and in its shade rest three big pots of white marguerites, plus two smaller ones filled with lilliputian members of the chrysanthemum family (*palusosum*), a white daisy that stands eight inches tall. It is important to always consider proportion by matching the height of a plant to the size of the container. Raising violets in one of those huge, converted wine barrels looks as funny as tucking a baby into a king-size bed. Here and there a single brick has been pried loose to plant patches of impatiens, a

stand of poppies, or penstemon. As for the lobelia, sweet alyssum, and feverfew, well the wind and birds drop their seeds in the terrace cracks. Each year, more and more bricks seem held together with blue, white, and yellow mortar.

When we bought the house, there was a magnificent giant of a Live California oak standing in the middle of what is now the terrace and its ancient crown covered half the house with a green beret. It was the one thing about the place that did not need remodeling but, to our deep sorrow, it only waited until our arrival and then started slowly dying from the smog. Around the base of the oak there had been a low brick wall-bench. We divided this seating area into four arc-shaped sections by removing bricks and filling the holes with soil. Year-round these hold ferns and moss, among which are planted different, low-lying flowers, depending on the season of the year. A massive clump of white daisies occupies the space where the trunk of the oak had stood. With back and armrests of blooms, I guess you could call this truly a garden seat.

We originally purchased a tubular iron dining table, which stands in the center of the terrace, because it was sturdy enough to support some rather heavy tiles I had designed in the shape of sunflowers. However, instead of covering the whole top with them, a circle was left untiled in the center. To fill that hole, thirty inches in diameter, a tinsmith made a five-inch deep, galvanized container, with five small drainage holes in the bottom. This built-in centerpiece is changed twice a year. Around its circumference there is always a border of white sweet alyssum; but in the winter yellow violas are planted in the center and, come summer, Petite

marigolds. When time permits there is often a third arrangement planted in early spring: lobelia, Peruvian verbena, and the same border of alyssum. It is impossible to feel unhappy sitting with such colorful, fascinating company. Unlike many people, flowers rarely bore.

About twenty feet from where the tiled luncheon table stands, one can see another stage in my continuing campaign to make the terrace a functional gardening area, where flowering plants are contained without looking restrained. We wanted a place where

If It's Empty,

Plant It

we could sit or lie in the sun without having to bother about dragging chairs and lounges back and forth. The solution was a sunbathing sundial. Like spokes in a wheel, six brick benches radiate out from a hexagon hub, formed at the point of their convergence. One can move from pallet to pallet—upholstered pads keep them from being as hard as stone—following the path of the sun. In accordance with Haraszty's Law: "If it's empty, plant it," the hub was filled with topsoil and, depending on the season, is planted with marigolds, sweet alyssum, yellow violas, or pansies.

About the pansies, I only use those without faces in this planter and the other terrace containers, because I want pure colors in confined areas. That way the pots and tubs catch the eye. There is a boldness and strength in the visually simple. A multihued pansy is fascinating to look at by itself but, when there are many of them in a small space, the total effect is busy, diffuse. Remember, also, that at one time or another the terrace pots with yellow and white blooms are brought into the living room, as portable bouquets, and solid colors balance off all the multiflower embroidery in that section of the house.

Here and there between the spokes of the sun-bathing dial, single bricks were pried from the terrace deck and planted with everything from strawberries to Iceland poppies to digitalis. Visitors are constantly surprised to see a four-foot-high daisy bush growing out of one of these four-by-eight-inch holes. What they do not know, of course, is that the terrace was put down on a bed of sand and that only the outside row of bricks—the one that holds all the others wedged in place—is set in cement. When the roots of young plants work their way down through the layer of sand, they find cool, life-sustaining earth, which is not a bad protective covering for plant roots exposed to full sunshine.

❀ 3 ❀

Container Culture

Caring for the movable feasts of flowers on the terrace or for the stationary planters—the center of the tile table, the hub of the brick dial, etc.—involves different methods than those used in normal bed-gardening. If plants are to survive in a confined space, then you must compensate for their being removed from a normal environment and nature's protective ways. Moreover, when you mass flowers together in a limited area, they are competing with each other for nourishment. So that none will turn out losers, your feeding program should be a generous one. Stuffing a container with a shovel full of earth from the garden, no matter how fertile the dirt may be, just won't do. You have to make up for the loss of nutrients and the gradual change that takes place in the soil's chemical structure due to the repeated watering required by flowering plants in pots and in hanging baskets.

If you happen to be blessed with good, rich earth, then simply add a commercial fertilizer and something to maintain porosity, like sponge rock. Unfortunately, our local soil contains enough clay to stock every kindergarten in California. It's good for building

The Right Soil and Fertilizer for Potting

❀ 33

adobe houses, but using it for potting is deadly. Consequently, I purchase cleaned-up dirt at the nursery. Called Supersoil—every region has a brand-named equivalent—it comes in various size bags, but to save time and money I always buy the largest size and make one big batch of planter mix. Whatever is left over is stored in a thirty-gallon garbage can for future use. To every two-cubic-foot bag of Supersoil—gardeners with acceptable topsoil would dig up the same quantity—I add a one-pound coffee can full of Osmocote 18-6-12. This is a nutrient used by professional flower growers and nursery owners. Although it is more expensive than the usual fertilizers, Osmocote is stronger and its time-release pellets are so structured that one application lasts for eight to nine months. The final ingredient is four coffee cans full of vermiculite or sponge rock. Either of these will keep the container soil loose and at the same time help in the retention of moisture.

Watering Containers and Hanging Baskets

It goes without saying that newly planted pots and baskets must be thoroughly watered *immediately;* but there is no such simple rule about day-to-day watering. Every terrace, in the city or the country, has different sun conditions. Even on the same patio, not all spots receive equal amounts of shade and light or are subject to identical air currents. Furthermore, the size and composition of each container determines how long it can retain moisture. The soil in plastic, clay, and terra-cotta pots dries out at a slower speed than that encased in metal; so throw away any tin cans nursery plants came in. Under a hot sun, dirt in a glazed ceramic holder will bake faster than that in an unglazed one. A hanging wire basket gets thirstier faster than a suspended redwood planter.

In addition, there is the variable of how well a certain container drains. Often the hole, or holes, at the bottom are too big and water flows out as fast as you hose it in. Or the reverse can happen. Drainage vents become stopped up with corks of packed earth and tangled roots. In that case, the plants soon drown to death. Both excesses can be avoided by covering the drainage hole with small stones, or pieces of a broken clay pot, before filling the container with soil.

Confronted with all of these variables, there is only one sure way for the beginning gardener to know when a pot, basket, or tub needs watering: stick your finger into the soil and take a moisture reading. If it comes out damp, there is no need for further water. If the earth is dry—and test deep enough not to be fooled by morning dew—get out the watering can. After awhile, one becomes familiar with the requirements of each container and flowering plant, at which time dirty fingernails will be reduced to a minimum. Hanging baskets, the wire type lined with sphagnum moss, call for the most attention as all their surfaces are exposed to the sun and drying winds. Soak them very slowly, using one of those watering wands that you can attach to your hose, which can be found at garden supply stores. Often, the water will not seep through to all areas of the mossy sheath, so it is a good idea to also spray the outside of these baskets with your hose.

To guarantee year-around color in a strategically located hanging basket, place an empty clay pot in its center, after you have lined the mesh with sphagnum moss and before filling in the soil around the middle container. Then, substitute a pot in full bloom for the empty one, repeating the process whenever the center flowers die off. Your substitution pots must all be the same size, of course. I hide all signs of fakery by growing moss or lobelia around the lip of the inserted container. Since hanging baskets are another kind of portable bouquet that can be brought inside for brief periods to dress up the house, this simple way of replacing the faded with the fresh is doubly convenient.

One last word about hanging containers. Because of the porous

Feeding and
"Faking"
Hanging
Baskets

———————

nature of their wire frames, pellet-type fertilizers are watered out of the soil. Consequently, it is best to use a liquid fertilizer, applied slowly, slowly, slowly. Do it every three to four weeks during the growing season for lush, full blooms. But, I find that even these precautions are not enough and twice, every year, each basket is taken down and soaked for several hours in a laundry tub filled with a water and fish emulsion solution. Those are the two days when we can count on our three cats never leaving the terrace area.

One of the nicest things about working with portable and container bouquets is that you do not have to lean over backward—or forward, which is more to the point—to keep the plants in shape. They are conveniently near the house and are usually elevated to within arms' reach. With morning coffee in one hand, I wander about the terrace admiring the day's new flowers and snipping faded blossoms. This habit of peripatetic plant care has become so automatic that I often find myself pinching off a dead geranium or cleaning yellow leaves from a hanging fuchsia while a guest in someone else's patio.

Containers Make Pest Control Easy

With a garden so near at hand there is really no excuse for not noticing the first signs of aphids and mildew, two plant ravagers most easily stopped in their early stages. Have your nursery dealer keep you informed of the latest nonpoisonous insecticides, those least likely to tip nature's scale of checks and balances. The systemic liquids and powders, which work from within a plant's stem and leaf structure, are effective for most common blights and fungi. Actually, our terrace plantings and baskets are usually relatively free of bugs. Most years, ladybugs, birds screened out of the vegetable garden, and our probing fingers are able to eliminate uninvited pests.

With the amount of watering, cleaning, feeding, showering, and dusting that goes on outdoors, container arrangements brought into the house are neat guests who do not require too much tidying up after. For the heavier tubs, once it is put down—that's it. Therefore, prior to the lugging of big pots and tubs, large woven baskets are placed in the exact spot I want to lower my burden. I can fetch and shift about the smaller ones with greater flexibility. We have a friend who has simplified the whole process. She scrounged her way through dozens of antique shops, looking for something or other to hold a collection of flowering pots on her terrace. It had to have wheels for indoor trips. She finally settled on a Victorian wicker baby carriage—for twins.

I have complicated my own interior use of outdoor planters by painting all of the latter a deep, rich blue. The color looks wonderful on the terrace, but blue pots on a yellow tile floor or next to a shocking pink chaise are hardly a happy juxtaposition of colors. So to avoid such clashes, I have accumulated baskets and cachepots in every possible size and shape. Almost all of them are very simple in design and neutral in color, since one's eye should go to the living flower arrangement, not to its holder.

Unfortunately, pottery makers and basket weavers don't seem to communicate with each other. Either that or one group has switched to the metric system before the other, for it is almost impossible to locate a holder that properly fits around standard size clay pots. Between the inside rim of the first and the outer edge of the second, there always seems to be an awkward gap of several inches. To hide this misfit, stuff sphagnum moss in the top of the fissure and carry the green cover (it will turn from brown to green with watering), over the lip of the pot and onto the soil area. If done carefully, it will seem as though the outer basket is your sole planter. Better still, the sphagnum serves more than merely a cosmetic purpose. Stretched around the plants, it helps the earth retain moisture when exposed to a house's unnaturally dry atmosphere. To avoid water-stained floors and table tops, do not forget to place a saucer—with an inch of #1 rock, for moisture retention—at the bottom of each basket before putting in the portable bouquet.

Big Rewards from a Small Greenhouse

This section on live flower arrangements would not be complete were I not to mention the wondrous off-season floral pleasures that can come out of a personal greenhouse. I know the phrase sounds very grand and expensive, like having a sauna house of one's own; but for the past few years there have been portable greenhouses on the market, selling for around one hundred and fifty dollars. The one we have is made of heavy-duty, transparent plastic, stretched over a modular frame and measures four by six feet. Six feet, six inches at the center beam, one person can stand and work at the potting shelves. It is small enough to fit on a city terrace, and the structure is sufficiently roomy to house a good supply of flowering plants during the winter months. The manufacturers sell add-on units for those who become seriously involved with greenhouse horticulture.

First off, it serves as an intensive-care ward for houseplants in need of rest and rehabilitation. Then, there is one shelf in the greenhouse devoted entirely to tiny plants and seeds being babied along until they are hardy enough to face the outside world, such as fuchsia. I can purchase all the major strains in four-inch pots for under one dollar at the local supermarket. After three months of nursing, forced feeding, and transplanting to larger pots, they are ready for inclusion in a hanging basket, about the size of one that would cost at least twenty dollars in a plant shop. Do this a dozen times and you have paid for the greenhouse.

Using peat moss pots (they decompose in the soil), I raise corn and green peppers from seed in the greenhouse. That way, as soon as the ground is warm enough—when night temperatures are over fifty degrees Farenheit—for planting, I am able to put in shoots that are already several weeks old. You can give tomato and cucumber plants the same sort of head start.

I also depend upon our greenhouse to carry certain flowering plants through their dormant period, like the four white phalaenopsis, which stand in a cluster on our dining area table. When they have shed the last of their lovely white blossoms, I cut back the stems to just below the spot where the lowest flower has been and let them rest until the following year. They need a warm place to hibernate so, what with our often frosty nights, the greenhouse is their sole, safe refuge. However, for those in a cold climate, a greenhouse usually makes the difference between having and not having flowering plants in the house from late fall to early spring. I say "usually" for there are always live bouquets to be had during off-season at the florist. Of course, you'll be had too.

If we ever move back East—something we sometimes talk about, particularly when the temperature is ninety degrees on a Christmas Day—I know the last object to go into the van, and the first possession unloaded, will be the greenhouse. Should such a moment come, I guess I will then order another greenhouse wing for, in addition to forcing all sorts of bulbs, I plan on raising live bouquets that contain geraniums, primroses, begonias, hydrangeas, gloxinia, cineraria, mums, and African violets. When that first white Christmas blankets the landscape, I want our home to be full of hothouse colors.

4

Morning Harvest

I am always amused by certain occasional visitors who rhapsodize over "all the magnificent flowers in your garden" yet, when I suggest that they collect an armful to take home, they look as though I had just extended an invitation to participate in genocide. They feel that the blooms are too pretty to pick and that the look of the garden would be spoiled. I try to explain why the garden will die off, if they are *not* picked. A plant's life cycle is geared toward one goal: reproduction. They grow to blossom, then go to seed. When the last step occurs, if it is a perennial, the plant is finished for the year; and if an annual, finished forever. Therefore, when flowers are cut regularly, the plants keep striving to produce seed-bearing blossoms. In short, the more you pick, the longer your garden will stay in bloom.

For me, flower picking is the most peaceful time of my day. I do not have to talk or think. Like a cat rolling over in a patch of catnip, I just luxuriate in all the exciting sights and smells around me. My only problem is greed. I have to force myself not to fly from flower to flower, like a bee. The simplest pleasures seem to call for the most discipline.

Were I not an incorrigible late riser, I would be out gathering flowers very early in the morning, when they are fresh from a night's rest and washed in dew. As it is, I just make it out of bed in time to rescue them from the sun's first hot rays, at about nine o'clock. On a foggy or overcast morning, they might not see me until ten. To make up for my belated attention, the flowers are gathered before I have had breakfast. One can also gather the makings of a bouquet late in the day, at dusk. When that time is more convenient, I always place the cut flowers in a deep container and let them stand in a cool place, overnight, with their heads just above water level. That way, they are still garden fresh when it comes to arranging them the following morning.

Even with something as simple as picking a flower, there is a right way and a wrong. Do not twist, snap, tear, bend, or pull off a flower from its plant. A stem must be cleanly severed if it is to function as the feeding channel for the cut blossom.

Thin stems, like those on Iceland poppies and pansies, may be snipped off between thumbnail and first finger, while the thicker, pulpy stalks of tulips, iris, Shasta daisies, etc., call for a pair of scissors. There is a type on the market that cuts and holds on to the severed stem with each snip, but I prefer the heavier, ordinary scissor, the kind used for cutting string and paper. If they are big enough, sharp enough, and sturdy, they will do just fine. On the other hand, when you are gathering woody-stemmed flowers like roses, lilacs, and flowering fruits and leafy branches, a pair of special pruning shears is essential. They are sold in all hardware and nursery stores and you will find that their curved blades are also helpful in cutting heavy-stalked sunflowers, Canterberry bells, and hollyhocks. Since pruning shears have to be sent out several times a year for professional sharpening, I keep a second pair in reserve. Also, like my glasses, I invariably mislay one set for two or three days at a stretch.

Speaking of pairs, next to the scissors and clippers on my work table is a stack of ninety-nine-cent white cotton work gloves. For a long time, I resisted wearing the cumbersome things, thinking they smacked of Helen Hokinson garden clubs and floppy gardening hats. More important, what was the fun of working with flowers if you could not experience the tactile pleasures of fuzzy stems, silky petals, and cool, damp earth. But, after several years of working bare-handed, I woke up one morning with what looked like a textbook case of measles. Hands, arms, neck, and face were swollen and each of the countless red spots itched. Our doctor took one look and rerouted me to the hospital. After forty-eight hours of ice-packed sedation, they announced that I had probably developed an allergy to something in the garden, which did not exactly pinpoint my problem. Rather than go through endless lab tests to find the poisonous needle in an acre and a half of haystack, I bought a dozen pair of gloves and a dozen tubes of allergy cream. After about a year of periodic scratching, I was finally able to put object and itch together. The villains were, and are, roses, daisies, and pine needles.

Different Flowers Call for Different Cutting Methods

Naturally, now, I do not feel compelled to fill the house with fresh arrangements every day of the year; but from midwinter to early July, I do gather the Iceland poppies first thing each morning to assure a continuous and bountiful supply of new blooms. My method in picking these favorites can be followed with most other flowers. To protect the plant, always snip the stems as close to the ground as possible. Roses and flowering shrubs are the exception to this rule. The first is normally cut, on a forty-five-degree angle, just above the next emerging shoot. On new rose bushes, do not be so severe. Give them a chance to start, to get their strength, to establish their crowns.

The same regard for age must be shown with flowering shrubs. If a stand of forsythia or snowball is mature and well established, then trim off branches to suit your needs; but always take into consideration how the plucked shrub is going to look. Pick and prune at the same time, shaping as you go. Select branches that are out of line with their neighbors or lone offshoots straggling around the base. By doing this housekeeping while gathering flowers, you are saving yourself a return trip to prune. The same sort of cleaning up can be done when picking any kind of flower. Dead or infested leaves and faded blossoms should be pinched off. I do not want to take all the fun out of harvesting flowers by suggesting too many side chores, but as long as you are bent over, pick a weed or two, while you can still extract them without a tug-of-war.

Back to those morning sessions among the poppies: as with all other flower varieties but one, I try to pick them half-open or in their bud stage to insure a longer life indoors. The "but one" in my garden are the zinnias. They can only be cut when fully opened, if you want them to last. I once tested the indoor life span of Iceland poppies and found that those that had been gathered when the first trace of color showed through their fuzzy, green casing lasted two to three days longer than the ones picked without jackets. Do not worry about having to look at a pitcher full of closed flowers for very long. Poppies pop open in the course of a day, an escape trick I never tire of watching. To further assure a long life for these magnificent blooms, char the cut ends of their stems over a gas burner. If your stove is electric, then use a candle flame to singe them. This clears out the gum that, unless removed, blocks the intake of water. The only other flower that calls for a similar trial by fire is the poinsettia.

Normally, before setting out to collect flowers, I wander through the house, deciding which arrangements need freshening and where new bouquets will go. Then, when I am actually picking, I keep in mind the basic color scheme of each room. There is nothing complicated about the system and I do not want to seem like an interior decorator matching swatches or using phrases like "color coordinated." It is simply that certain colors go well together *for me,* others do not. I will get into these complementary combinations in Chapter 8, but, for the moment, it is enough to explain that *our* house is broken up into different color areas. There are warm yellows and bright oranges in the living room and adjacent dining area; all the embroidered furniture, the couch, the skylight shade, and the rug in the plant-filled solarium stress shades of red; the bedroom, master bath, and kitchen are filled with cool, peaceful blues. When out in the garden, I think of these backgrounds and select flowers accordingly.

A goodly part of the morning's bounty always lands in what I call the living kitchen, an around-the-clock meeting and eating place for us, our close friends, and pets. In keeping with the countrylike feeling of the room, an ironstone pitcher on the oak dining table is filled with one huge bunch of poppies, while an earthenware butter crock near the telephone holds the short-stemmed part of the harvest—as some people may doodle during dull phone conversations, I prefer to help a few poppies out of their green jackets. There is no reason why both of us have to feel trapped. Two or three of the reddest "Champagne Bubble" variety, the largest and strongest of the Iceland poppies, are placed in an old blue glass bottle for the master bath and, finally, a large bunch of them is always within view of where I'm working, either on the drafting table in my studio or beside the study couch where I embroider each evening. No person or thing has had more influence on my creative output while in California than the Iceland poppy.

Before allowing my favored poppies to distract me from the business at hand, I was talking about knowing what color blossoms you need before setting out to pick them. In the same fashion, predetermining the size of flowers you will be using saves repeated trips to the garden. Even more time consuming is wandering around the house with a finished arrangement in your hands that seems either too high or too low for any possible location. Scale and proportion are as important as color in the placement of flowers. However, your bouquets will not seem out of place if you follow a simple rule: tall flowers belong next to large objects.

Think of Scale when Choosing Which to Cut

In our living room, for example, in front of a tile-topped console is a big Victorian sofa, flanked by a pair of end tables. Tall and full flower arrangements always stand on these side tables, because I want to minimize the expanse of sofa; dominate large pieces of furniture with large floral displays. If flowers cannot be the winner in such a battle, at least settle for nothing less than a draw, for only then will the objects in a room blend into a harmonious whole. I love good antiques as well as the clean lines of modern, but there is no reason why, upon entering a house, a person's eyes should be made to bounce from one "important" object to another. That kind of show-off decorating is best restricted to museums, auction galleries, furniture showrooms, and San Simeon.

Sometimes an imposing group of flowers serves to divert attention from something a lot more formidable than a Victorian sofa. That table console, I just mentioned, is attached to an eight-by-eight-inch column in the center of the living room. A source of constant annoyance, we would have gotten rid of the eyesore years ago, except that a contractor warned us against being impetuous since it holds up the ceiling and the roof. I always stand a large

Screening with Bouquets

particularly colorful bouquet on the console, right up against the column. That does not help people to see around the column, but it does have a way of bedazzling their vision so that they look no farther.

Utilizing a
Natural Place
for Cut
Flowers

In front of the living room fireplace is a round marble table, four and one-half feet in diameter and a foot and a half high; just far enough off the floor for the dogs to crawl under. It is the gathering place for after-dinner coffee, cocktails, sit-on-the-floor midnight suppers, fire watching, and talk sessions. It is the visual as well as social center of the room and, therefore, a natural place for cut flowers. Since the table is low, I think small when gathering blossoms for the spot in order not to throw the setting out of balance. A bowl of short-stemmed roses, a nosegay of yellow violas, or a snowy mound of white sweet peas would be in the right scale. I must keep two other things in mind when preparing these arrangements. The table's surface has to remain free for the paraphernalia of entertaining. There are always ash trays, cigarette boxes, and match holders on the marble top and, at one time or another, cocktail glasses, decanters, trays of canapes, and so on. Moreover, people sitting on the floor should be able to see who they are talking to across the table.

Despite these restrictions I have fun with the flower arrangements for this table. I play with the scale. Sometimes I'll group together three or four different size flower containers—from a three-inch mercury glass bud holder to a very slim, art nouveau vase a foot tall—and place a few extra special blossoms in each, perhaps anemones, California poppies, some ranunculi, or a single cabbage rose. Never forget that less is sometimes more and that in a lone bloom there is often the suggestion of a whole garden of beauty.

Now that I have laid down some general rules about picking and placing flowers, let me break one of them. I can start a flower-gathering session determined to be organized and disciplined, to harvest by color and by size; but, while I am picking, something often happens to disrupt all those good intentions. A sudden breeze may ruffle across a bed, bending two different flowers together in a color combination I had never thought of using before; or the sun, shining through a stand of daisies, may cast a shadow on the brick walk, which makes me think of a new shape for an arrangement. Usually, it is nothing specific that inspires the creative process but, whenever it happens. I head back to the house with a basket full of flowers entirely different than those I set out to gather. The bouquet I compose from these "impulse" cuttings will be as good as my ability to understand and translate into visual terms the momentary insight I had been given by nature. Maybe such an unpremeditated flower arrangement will not precisely fit the place where you needed color, but it is bound to find a home in some room of your house. A coupling of unplanned flowers can have very winning ways.

If you keep your mind open, as well as your eyes, more than merely flowers will be brought back from one of these collecting expeditions. Nature inspires in so many ways but, of equal importance, it also gives one the courage to attempt the untried. For instance bright colors: most Americans are afraid to use them in their homes, preferring the safer shades of brown, green, or blue. Ironically, color inhibitions seem strongest among those in cold climates. Think how being surrounded by pure, strong yellows, oranges, and reds would help warm a snowbound house. I've made a few converts among visitors from the East by taking them for a walk in the garden and letting the flowers do the talking. I re-

The

Unexpected

Arrangement

_____

member one very conservative friend asking me, "How do you think that would do back in Boston?" while looking at a stretch of California poppies growing among the citrus trees in the orchard. I answered, "They're a native wild flower out here. I don't think they could stand your climate."

"Oh, I wasn't thinking of growing them. I just want to redo our living room in those colors. What do you think?" From Boston-bean brown to vibrant yellow orange; I was delighted.

However, one should never expect an exact translation of the shades seen in a garden. We have all heard of the person who takes a cornflower into a fabric store or waves a chrysanthemum under a house painter's nose and says, "Match this." It cannot be done. Nature has her own unbreakable patents. In one rose petal, there are a dozen different hues, mixed together with another secret formula: sunlight. Trying to understand and reproduce these intangibles is what inspires, challenges—and ultimately frustrates—all artists. I am sure that that is partly what the eighteenth-century painter Holman Hunt had in mind when he wrote, "I feel really frightened when I sit down to paint a flower."

Fortunately, nature is open-handed with her other gifts. Every time I go outdoors to plant, to harvest, or simply to flower-watch, I learn a little more about the meaning of simplicity, balance, restraint, and harmony. These are the attributes of blooming beauty that I try to incorporate in every floral arrangement. I should quickly add that I also want the flowers in our home to engender surprise and humor, those two marvelous levelers of pretentiousness. To prove that I do not take myself too seriously, join me while I put together some bouquets in my working area.

❧ 5 ❧

Tools and Tricks
of the Trade

Flower arranging and cooking are similar in that they both leave a mess. And, for a while they both shared something else in our house, the kitchen. When I first started gardening, that was the room that seemed the most logical place to sort out the harvest. There was running water and two sinks next to a very large chopping block, which I could use as a worktable. The tile floor and counters made cleaning up a relatively simple chore. All in all, it is usually the most functional area in which to prepare cut flowers. I recommend it to everyone. However, in my case, when flower arranging became more than just a hobby, using a much trafficked and social part of the house as a professional workroom proved impractical. So, I moved my basket and bowls and tools to the back porch—which also served as the doghouse.

Perhaps the best way to describe the mechanics of flower arranging is to give a sort of dress rehearsal of the real thing. Let me set the stage, being sure all the necessary props are in place, the most important of which is a solid and spacious surface to work on. I use a bench made of old beams, leftovers from when the house

Adequate

Working

Space

❧ *49*

was being remodeled. A roomy kitchen counter or sturdy table will do as well. Every bouquet in my New York City days was put together in the small guest bathroom of my apartment with two boards placed across the top of the tub for a worktable.

To be sure that there is sufficient free space to work in, the only other items one should keep on the table, beside a large sponge and a roll of paper towels for cleaning up, are a pair of regular scissors and garden clippers. I depend on the latter two so often that they are really like a second pair of hands. See to it that their blades do not get dull—I have mine professionally sharpened regularly— because it is most important that stems and branches are cut cleanly. Ragged, torn ends will interfere with the flower's ability to draw water and scraggly stems are difficult to work into wire holders or blocks of Oasis. I hate having to waste time and interrupt the flow of ideas by looking in drawers and cabinets for equip-

ment; therefore, the relatively few things I need are kept on a nearby shelf. If you have no such free surface available, a basket or an ordinary tool box will do splendidly.

Don't Let the "Doing" Spoil the Fun or the Arrangement

Too much of a production can be made of what should be the natural, relaxed pursuit of a simple hobby. Particularly when an art form is involved—flower arrangements can rise to that level—overemphasis on mechanics and technique will lessen the feeling of spontaneity and freedom in the finished product. Nature seems effortless and it is that marvelous quality that every flower composition should reflect. If a cut flower has been bent by the wind or by a pushy neighboring plant, its inclusion in a bouquet will only enhance the natural appearance of the floral grouping; but I would never intricately wire a straight stem to make it bend or curve to my will. Which brings us back to the real reason why I cringe at the word *arrangement*. The contrived, the fabricated, will spoil the effect of a pitcher of blossoms more quickly than the absence of water.

The Wide and Useful World of Baskets

In the room where I work on my flowers, baskets dangle from hooks in the ceiling, hang on nails driven into wall studs, and are stacked in nests on shelves. As some women collect sweaters or shoes, I am a patsy for any interestingly shaped basket, be it fashioned from straw, bark, raffia, twigs, cane, rope, or bamboo. The more unusual the texture, the better. Their rough, woven surfaces and honest, unobtrusive colors make them ideal flower holders. Moreover, they come in so many different sizes that are just not available in pitchers and bowls.

Do not restrict yourself to the Little Red Riding Hood type with a handle. There are many other possibilities: I put pansies in a long, reed French bread holder; five-foot-high mimosa branches stand in a huge grape harvest basket; a partitioned wicker carrier

BASIC FLOWER-ARRANGING EQUIPMENT

1 Japanese saw	—shaped like a knife, it will cut through thick branches you cannot manage with garden clippers.
1 pair of garden clippers	—also known as pruning shears. They come in different sizes, so find one that fits your grip.
1 package of 18-gauge wire	—these lengths of thin wire have as many uses as a bobby pin.
1 box of Twist-'ems	—paper-covered wire that comes in a roll. Used to hold bouquets together.
1 pair of leather gloves	—for working with thorny flowers and branches.
1 pair of cotton gloves	—for those whose fingernails and hands are not past saving. I find them difficult to work in, but good protection from allergy-causing flora.
1 staple gun	—see section on lining baskets.
1 glue gun	—when a staple gun or tape won't do the job, this inexpensive device will; available in most hardware stores.
tissue paper	—several packages in white and different colors to wrap floral gifts.
heavy knitting yarn	—to tie the above presents.
1 box of plastic bags	—a drip-proof way to carry bouquets any distance, but first wrap the stems in wet paper towels to preserve freshness.
1 roll of paper towels	
1 spray bottle	—fill with water and use to mist finished flower arrangements.
1 hammer	—the simplest way to mash the ends of woody branches like forsythia, lilac, and snowball to aid water absorption.

Tools and Tricks of the Trade ≫53

1 box of Stickum	—a malleable substance—comes in green and white—which can be used to fasten decorations to Christmas trees, wreaths, bouquets, etc.
1 package of pipe cleaners	—when wet, they can be inserted into hollow stems to save broken or severely bent stems.
1 kitchen knife	—very sharp, medium size. An auxiliary tool to scissors and garden clippers. Perfect for stripping thorns from roses.
chicken wire	—buy the kind with one-inch holes. When rolled and moulded to fit inside of flower container, material makes a dependable holder for stems.
1 pair of wire cutters	—to work with the above.
needle holders	—looking like a "bed of nails," they come in rectangles and circles to fit the bottom of vases and bowls. I find them more trouble than they are worth, but that is definitely a minority opinion, so you had best try for yourself.
thick guage plastic	—the clear, heavy-duty type. Used in lining baskets and other porous containers.
aluminum foil	—a roll of the heavy-duty variety. Another way to wrap damp stems of flowers when in transit, also for use as a liner.
1 awl or ice pick	—for making holes in Oasis. A large carpenter's nail will do as well.
blocks of Oasis	—a flower-holding compound, placed at the bottom of containers. Usually white or green, it is water absorbent and can be cut to desired size with a knife.

Add a box of spring clips, rubber bands, a package of drinking straws, some old newspapers and that's it.

for six wine bottles can be used as a container for six different bouquets or for the same flower, say geraniums, in various shades. The French weave deep coasters out of twigs for wine bottles: these look like large bird nests, making charming individual flower holders for each place setting at a dinner table. I find some of my best baskets in shops that sell cooking and kitchen utensils.

Of course, this marvelous assortment of flower holders has one obvious and major drawback—they do not hold water. Leak-proof liners must be found to nest within the baskets. That is often easier said than done, but start the search by going to the kitchen cupboard. You may be lucky enough to locate a metal bread pan or a deep cake tin, a glass casserole, or some mixing bowls that fit the baskets you have on hand. Sometimes, a plain old pail fits snugly into a round wicker basket, or an aluminum foil roasting pan, turkey size, will take care of your square-shaped needs. Other pos-

Ready-made
Basket Liners
if You're
Lucky

Tools and Tricks of the Trade ❧ 55

sibilities in the same genre include: empty soup, coffee, or fruit juice cans, and wide-necked glass containers, like apple sauce and pickle jars. One solution is to build a supply of those plastic, food-storage containers in various sizes—round, square, and oblong—found in every supermarket and dime store.

Sometimes, though, neither your cupboards nor the store has the exact size of substitute liner required and that is when you make your own, as professional florists do.

How to Line a Container Simply and Professionally

The technique is quick and simple: Spread a single sheet of *heavy*-duty polyethylene—not the skimpy sandwich-bag type, but the thick variety found in most paint and hardware stores—over the top of the basket. If the inside of the latter is prickly with reed or cane ends, capable of pricking the plastic, first lay down a protective coating or two of aluminum foil. Then, gently push down the polyethylene until it covers the bottom of the container and is as flush as possible against its sides. Holding the plastic in position with one hand, use the other to fasten the sheathing with a staple gun to the lip of the basket. Should the rim be too fragile or too bulbous to take a staple, use small spring clips or a glue gun. Do this relining job well the first time and the converted basket will last for many refills. Also, you will find the heavy plastic easy to sponge clean after each use.

If you have ever closely examined the construction of a basket from a commercial florist you will know that this is basically the method they employ, using either chicken wire or Oasis wedged between the sides of the container to hold and support the flowers. The more expensive florists quite often use liners made of papier-mâché. Costing between 25¢ and $2.50 each, they come in many different sizes and their bottoms are coated with Lapp Cement—a durable, waterproof substance—permitting frequent reuse. Of course, these fillers are the ultimate solution to most lining needs; however, they are not always readily available to retail customers, nor do they come in the odd shapes some baskets call for.

This system of drip proofing may be used in those favorite flower bowls that have developed leaking, hairline cracks. Antiquity, however, is not always the sole reason that a holder drips or "sweats." Many of the wonderfully shaped pieces of earthenware pottery made in Mexico leak like southern California roofs—all the time. When confronted with one of these despoilers of wood patina and marble sheen, I first try coating its insides with a waterproof sealant, like Lapp Cement, sold at any hardware or paint store. Better still, and far safer, convert imperfect bowls into cachepots by slipping an empty produce or tobacco can, or a water glass, into the damaged container. The same first-aid procedure can often be followed with prized pitchers that have sprung a leak. Since part of the beauty and charm of native crafts and antiques is their irregularity, one must be prepared to accept their structural ones, also.

Making Old Flower Bowls Watertight

Once, in Mexico City, I found a two-handled, hooded basket for toting babies. Afraid it would be crushed in the plane's luggage compartment, I carried the crib—filled with ceramic booty—on my lap during the return trip to Los Angeles. Back home, there was a letter awaiting me from *McCall's* magazine, asking if I had any ideas for a photographic story on what to do with flowers at Christmas time. Having been in non-Christmasy California for several years, I had a lot; but my favorite picture among those published was the one of the raffia crib. Unable to find a holder that would match the basket's special dimensions, we hunted out the professional of last resort, a tinsmith. They will duplicate any shape in galvanized metal—tin eventually rusts—or copper. I

Special Order Basket Liners Made of Metal

chose the first, it being the most practical and cheapest. Then the holder and the crib were painted with flat white enamel and filled with sprays of wild berries, sprigs of holly, lemon and orange branches ripe with fruit, and cuttings from a fir tree. The grouping spoke of peace and God's gifts, things I wished for everyone but particularly for the Mexican peasants who had, in the first place, created such a joyful basket out of so very little.

All baskets need not be made of straw. About five years ago, a friend gave us a bread basket woven from strands of real bread dough. Afraid that the gift might break from frequent use, I placed it in the center of the dining table and—using an oblong Pyrex dish to hold the water—filled it with bouquets of short-stemmed blooms: geraniums, primroses, yellow and white daisies, pansies, etc. The centerpiece looked so lovely and fitting that I decided to create other dining accessories from flour and water. The idea oc-

Unusual

Flower

Holders, Made

from Flour

and Water

———————

PLATES 23

25

27

29

curred to me at one of those times when I had nothing but dead-line jobs to finish. Rather than put off the project to "another time," which usually means forever, I tracked down a professional baker who was willing to take the time to duplicate my designs for bowls, deep trays, and baskets with handles. I frequently use the first to hold fruits and vegetables decorated with the plants from which they come, say lemons or strawberries nestled in a bed of their own leaves or onions interspersed with the pincushionlike onion flower. For the fun of it, you may go even further botanically by coupling different fruits and blossoms that are from the same family, i.e., strawberries with roses or *solanum* blooms with pota-toes and tomato. The circular tray with a braided rim is some-times put in the center of our coffee table and filled with different types and sizes of white daisies, cut so that they form a snowy mount.

Naturally, there is no reason to have these bread containers

made by a professional; besides, as I subsequently discovered when not pressed for time, you miss all the fun of molding and baking them yourself. Here is a dependable recipe for those who wish to sculpt with baker's clay:

INEDIBLE DOUGH

4 cups of unsifted, all-purpose flour
1 cup of salt
1 ½ cups of water

Mix all three ingredients thoroughly in a bowl. If dough is too stiff to handle, add additional water, a bit at a time. Knead on a flour-dusted board for five or six minutes, then form to desired shape using an upside down Pyrex or metal dish as your form. Place both in a preheated oven (350° F) and bake for 1 hour or more, depending on the thickness and size of your basket. Test with a toothpick in thickest part of design. When no part of dough is soft, remove from oven to allow to cool. Once at room temperature, baskets may be painted if you wish, although I prefer the natural look. Then spray them with Hyplar (made by M. Grumbacher, Inc., New York City, and available in art supply stores), a plastic varnish coating that keeps out bugs and moisture and gives the finished basket a dust-proof sheen.

NOTE: 1) Dough must be used within four hours or it will become too dry. 2) The safest way to affix a

handle to a basket is to mold it around a wire support. 3) Just like a first cake, your initial basket may flop. Keep trying until you get the formula right. 4) The metal or glass form on which you baked the basket can subsequently serve as its waterproof liner. 5) This recipe should not be cut in half.

Caution: Baskets and bowls made of even the thickest dough are fragile, especially their bottoms, which crack or break under any but the lightest weight. Therefore, always place the baked container where you want it *empty,* then fill it up with the flowers, fruits, or vegetables of your choice.

After espousing bread baskets in this fashion, I should make it quite clear that I am not of the school—although it seems to have more graduates than all others combined—that believes anything that can be made to hold water is appropriate to use for flowers. I am after a contemporary, fresh approach to flower arranging and some of the familiar container clichés are not in harmony with that goal. So many commonly used holders are, for me, contrived, gimmicky, or cute and their falseness destroys the naturalness of the flowers they support. Some examples of the contrived: those very low rectangular and square receptacles, the ones you have to load down with mechanical devices to make a bouquet stand up; a perched funnel-shaped cup in the top of a candlestick that is to hold blossoms. Or what about the practice of using bowls and compotes with built-in pedestals? If I want height, I achieve the effect with flowers. As for the gimmicky and cute, atop my list go all "gift shop" ceramics made in the shape of shoes, boots, hats, household furnishings, and domestic pets. I feel nearly as embarrassed when

Contrived Holders Will Ruin the Most Beautiful Flowers

confronted with floral arrangements draped around decapitated statues or smiling figurines. But for the height of silliness, I would have to choose the example of innovative container use illustrated in a recent book on arrangements. A bouquet sprung from the top coils of an automobile spring that had been anchored to stand on the perpendicular. Better to save one's imagination for the selecting of flowers than to waste it on their container.

You Will End Up Using the Simplest Containers the Most

My own choice of flower holders has always been governed by a desire for the functional in harmonious, yet interesting, shapes. Familiar forms are more important than "eye catchers," and pure, bright colors predominate. The following inventory of the containers I use most shows that one need not spend a fortune to build up a varied and adequate collection. Also, you will notice that many of them moonlight from other duties.

When using the more conventional pitchers and bowls, it is nice that so many of them invoke special memories. If I do not return from a journey with "something for the flowers," you can be sure that it was strictly a business trip. In the summer of

A Baedeker of Pottery and Memories

1972, we drove to Cape Cod and back, our first real vacation since moving to California. The journey was made at a leisurely pace and there was time for the wonders of a vast land to register. And time for a little pottery puttering. I think of the early morning, woodsy silence along the crest of the Blue Ridge Mountains whenever I reach for an off-white, rough-glazed pitcher bought at a roadside cooperative run by Appalachian artisans. In the town of Paris, Tennessee, I found the most authentic American, little brown jug this side of the Smithsonian, which turned out to have been made in Japan. Coming across the southwestern part of the nation, we stopped at a tiny Indian village, perched atop a thousand-foot-high mesa. There I purchased a fertility vase, a sort

CONTAINERS

Enamel kitchenware: Water pitchers, coffee and tea pots, soup tureens, drinking cups, milk pails. Those made in Japan, and readily available, come in wonderfully clear colors, good shapes. Inexpensive.

Copper and brass: Cooking containers, including stock pots, hot milk servers, cake molds, Turkish coffee pots, old-fashioned milk delivery cans, deep mixing bowls, elongated fish poacher. Those imported from France have the most classic lines.

Glass: Crystal bud vases from the Scandinavian countries. Large, wide-mouthed, long-stemmed red wine goblets. Tulip-shaped champagne glasses. Ice buckets. Every possible size and shape of pitcher, from a small creamer to party-size beverage containers. Apothecary jars and bottles. Antique herb jars. The old nickle beer glasses, wine carafes, mugs. Miniature liquor bottles and some of the wonderfully designed gallon and half-gallon jugs being used by California wine makers (Paul Masson, Gallo, and Giumarra are the best, bottles, that is). French bistro wine tumblers. Small, mercury glass vases. A few tall glass vases, preferably simple, trumpet-shaped ones; for their narrow bases hold stems in place, while the wide mouths allow blossoms to flow up and out in freedom.

A personal note about the above items: unless I can find a marvelous true blue or some of those beautiful old hand-blown windowpane tints, I prefer not using colored glass containers. They either pale when in the company of nature's colors or stage a distracting, losing battle for who gets the attention. An exception to this rule is a pure

Tools and Tricks of the Trade ✄ 63

orange glass bowl by Venini, which I brought back from Venice.

Ceramic: An art nouveau porcelain vase. Victorian china, ironstone, and spatterware wash bowls and pitchers. Earthenware mugs, cups, and pitchers. Peasant pottery. Porcelain milk and cream containers. Early American pickling jars, stone bottles, cider and maple syrup jugs. Italian and French glazed cachepots, white or cream in a basket-weave design. Old Spanish bowls and pitchers, most of which have simple horizontal or vertical stripes. A French vitrified porcelain mortar. Turn-of-the-century English aspic and dessert molds.

Miscellaneous: Watering cans. Large, Dijon mustard pots. Wooden cheese molds from Holland. A Finnish sauna bucket made of birch. Two Sheffield wine coolers.

of double-tubed bud vase, one half-joined to the other by a gracefully arched handle. The first red and near-white poppies of
spring always end up in this twin holder.

And then there are pieces from abroad. The translucent orange
bowl from Venice (marigolds in the living room); three eighteenth-
century blue and white vases from Barcelona (cornflowers for the
bedroom), and a 1974 small milk pitcher, also blue and white, from
a hotel in Protofino (red roses by our bedside); three white water
pitchers (ranunculus, tithonia, and tulips, any room in the house),
each a different size but very simple and modern in design, plus a
pine sauna bucket (potted red and shocking pink geraniums, next
to the bathroom tub), all from Finland. In the mid-sixties, after a
twenty-years-later return to Hungary, I came back to America with
a few pieces of peasant pottery (mums, black-eyed Susans, and
daffodils in the study) and a great many shattered memories. On a

happier note, there is one flower container that never fails to make me smile: a small watering can, about four inches high. Made from a gas station's discarded Bardahl can, it must have been a child's plaything. My husband found the toy among a street vendor's wares in Guadalajara. This bit of unintentional pop art has a niche of its own in the kitchen and is usually filled with violets, the first crocus, a tiny cluster of Johnny-jump-up, or, as in this photograph of miniature European daises and parsley.

The Storage of Empty Pitchers, Vases, and Bowls

The flower-arranging room is a very functional place to work but there is little space, and no safety, there for my collection of pitchers and bowls. These stand on two deep shelves below a bay window in the living room. Since each item was selected for its pleasing shape and design, there is no reason for hiding them away in closets when they are not in use. Considering my habit of furnishing each area according to a particular color family, certain receptacles look out of place in the basically yellow living room. Consequently, empty containers in blue are scattered about the bedroom for their purely decorative value. In the accompanying photographs, you will find very few of the traditional glass, or silver, flower holders. To my way of thinking, there is nothing particularly attractive about watching a tangle of stems and leaves slowly decompose in murky water. The sight always reminds me of an aquarium in need of pool service. As for silver, it is a bit too sedate and formal for our way of life and my relaxed approach to floral displays; however, we do have two Sheffield wine buckets, which are polished up and filled with blossoms on special occasions: a midnight supper party, Christmas, or a New Year's Eve celebration. Silver, candlelight, and white flowers are a very festive trio. I must confess that if I did not hate cleaning silver, those wine coolers might be used more often.

What you will notice, though, in the book's pictures is that I rely heavily on various size pitchers for my arrangements. This is because their narrow tops and necks serve to hold a grouping of flowers together loosely and naturally, which is the ideal way for a bouquet to look in a container. Moreover, the individual blossoms are kept in place without having to resort to artificial holders at the bottom of the pitcher, those store-bought gimmicks made of wire, glass, or tiny metal prongs. These supposedly weighted devices have an infuriating way of slipping sideways and turning over. Also, there never seem to be enough holes or spikes in them for the number of flowers I wish to include in an arrangement. Just as distressing, affixing stems one by one to such holders, more often than not results in a stiff and studied composition of flowers, where each stem is uniformly distant from the next. Flowers were never meant to fall into a precise, symmetrical pat-

Why Bouquets
Look So Well
in Pitchers

tern. If nonconformity is rebellious, then nature was the first rebel.

Knowing my weakness for offbeat containers, an imaginative friend gave me a metal bicycle basket, circa 1925, which she found in some tiny English village. The beautifully proportioned accessory had obviously also been used for market shopping, since a very sturdy, wooden handle arched across the top. I decided to give it a third identity, that of a live and portable flower holder. You may do the same thing with any flat-bottomed wire container, like the hanging baskets used to drip-dry salads and rinse vegetables. Be sure your selection is sturdily made, however.

While Irish moss was used to line the present from England, I have done the same thing to other containers with baby's tears. Both of these creepers are available in flats at your garden center, which simplifies the following process: first, gently using a wide spatula, cut and lift wide strips of the plant. I stress delicacy, since both Irish moss and baby's tears have a shallow root system. You want a thin layer of the greenery, yet one with the roots in tact and undamaged. Next, line the four sides and bottom of the basket with the Irish moss, green side toward the wire mesh. Now you place a two-inch layer of sphagnum moss, which has been thoroughly soaked in water and squeezed out, against the root surface of the creeper. Holding the sphagnum firmly in place around the walls of the basket, you then proceed to fill the latter with good planting soil. Pat the earth down and soak it well, thus creating a sideways pressure, which will keep the sphagnum-backed Irish moss against the sides of the basket.

Unless the Irish moss and baby's tears are kept constantly moist during California's summer heat, it will die off, just as neither of them can survive an eastern winter unless placed in a greenhouse. So, to guarantee that the holder stays verdant year-round, I plant different types of small-leaf Hahn ivy (Sweetheart, Needlepoint, or Crested) in the soil, along the inside perimeter of the basket. Once these eight shoots root—you can plant more if you're in a rush for a green cover—and take hold, the trailers can be trained along the edges of the basket and down over the sides to be interwoven in wire mesh. As you can see, two of my ivy settings were coaxed along until they covered the handle on the bicycle basket. Of course, very patient gardeners who do not mind waiting at least a year for their container to be completely dressed in ivy green, may forget about starting off with Irish moss or baby's tears as an interim cloak. Turning the sheathed container into a receptacle for cut flowers is the easiest part.

Simply remove enough of the center soil to leave room for the insertion of two, four, or six empty four-inch plastic pots. Now, to decorate the basket with cut flowers, place glasses or jars in the plastic pots to serve as vases, but should you wish to use live plants—primula, cineraria, cyclamen, dwarf calendula, or whatever—substitute their holders for the ones sunken into the dirt. The floral carryall can then be toted to any section of the house in need of cheering up, like the portable bouquets in Chapter 2. Keep these containers outdoors in the shade when not in use, spray them with the hose often, and, to preserve their lush appearance, every six to eight weeks let the containers soak in a sink or laundry tub filled with a solution of liquid fertilizer and water. Finally, to maintain the original lines of the basket, every so often give a haircut to the green wrapper.

During occasional three-hour drives to the Mexican border and Tijuana, my eyes are always searching for new shapes in pitchers and bowls. Invariably, when I find something I want, it is decorated in garish day-glo colors or art tourista designs; nevertheless,

I shut my eyes and pay the few dollars, knowing that two coats of white acrylic will eradicate any number of stylized birds chirping "souvenir of Mexico." There are so many graceful containers ruined with paintings that any kindergarten student could improve upon; I am surprised that more people are not inspired to erase and then repaint these otherwise useful pieces of ceramic.

Actually, I guess I am not really surprised, having heard time and time again, "Oh, I could never paint a picture like you do. I'm not an artist." However put, the disclaimer is a cop-out. You do not have to be a trained artist to paint alternating bold stripes on a *One Way to* dingy mug or trace a simple pattern with the use of carbon paper. *Personalize a* Often the containers themselves provide guidelines as to what can be done. I am speaking of those ceramics that have relief work *Pitcher or* provided by the potter. It can be a raised band in a geometric *Bowl* design, a scattering of intaglio motifs, perhaps on ornate cartouche, or there may be a restrained pattern of ridges, ripples, concentric circles, or wavy lines. Try painting this relief work with a color, or colors, of which you are fond. "Trying" often turns out to be the difference between hoping and succeeding. Remember, if the finished decoration is not to your liking, a can of white paint is a foolproof eraser.

It once took me two solid weeks to paint Iceland poppies on what had been a Tijuana monstrosity. However, I finally managed to capture a little of the texture and colors that I love so much about those flowers. Perhaps, because some of the love shows, the poppy pitcher is among my favorite possessions. It stands in the center of the living room mantel and is always filled with its namesake. Should you still be worried that picking up a paint brush will lead PLATE 32 to disaster, take a look at the photograph of the blue and white

70 ⊰ *Living with Flowers*

delphiniums. They stand in what was once a two-quart produce basket, the kind you see on roadside vegetable stands. The shape, size, and familiar profile of these traditional containers seemed just right for informal flower arrangements. However, while I liked their functional appearance, the unfinished pine lath from which they are made was overly rustic, too Early Orange Crate for our house. The solution was elementary do-it-yourself. Since pine is so absorbent, the outside and inner lip of each basket was given three coats of quick-drying white. Then, depending on which part of the house they were intended for, the spaces between the horizontal bands were painted red, blue, or yellow. If you wish, it is the narrow bands that can be the second color. Once the baskets are dry, small plastic paint pails were slipped in as liners. Now you do not even have to try, to achieve that sort of a transformation.

In the same delphinium picture, you will notice a small blue and white lidded jar. It comes from Bologna, Italy, and once held brandied fruit. Therein lies another answer to the continually nagging question, "What shall I put the flowers in?" When twenty-first-century historians look back to judge the quality of our art, they may very well decide that ours was the age of the advertising art director, especially when their graphic talents were applied to food products in American and particularly abroad. What is inside today's cans and jars may not live up to some of the appetizing labels, but the latter can be a feast for the eyes. Take oatmeal, for instance. I'd rather not, but I am willing to suffer through a week or two of gluey porridge to own an empty can of John McCann's Irish Oatmeal, festooned with all the gold medals it has won at such places as the World's Columbian Exhibition, Chicago 1893, and the London Exhibition of 1851, when Prince Albert bestowed the awards. But far more delightful, internally that is: Bassermann's

A Produce Basket for a Harvest of Delphiniums

———————

Flower Holders That Were Made for the Kitchen

———————

PLATE 34

Tools and Tricks of the Trade ⊰ 71

two-pound pail of fresh plum jam. You do not have to read German to understand what ripe, sweet delights rest under the lid. Three purple plums on a golden-leafed vine tell the story.

The best packaging so far, though, is the five-pound tin of Amaretti Di Saronno macaroons made in Milan by D. Lazzaroni. PLATE 39 Aside from being illustrated with a king's ransom of gold and silver awards, the container is emblazoned with: heraldic devices; a trademark that is made up of an anchor, a wreath, lots of fluttering ribbons, and the picture of a paddlewheel sailing ship that has the biggest smog-spewing smokestack to ever sail the seven seas; a steel engraving of the Lazzaroni biscuit factory looking at least 150 years old; clusters of wheat and sprays of ivy. Why the six sides— yes, the bottom is illustrated, too—of the tin is a complete survey course in the history of Italy's Industrial Revolution. But most wonderful of all are those habit-forming macaroons. If my stomach had the say, every flower arrangement in the house would rest in one of these red and orange cans from Milan. Fortunately, it does not. Food cans are kept in their proper place, the kitchen.

Once Shirley MacLaine and Richard Nixon established détente between Red China and the United States, a store in Los Angeles began stocking merchandise from The Peoples' Republic of China. True to form, I immediately went shopping for vases, but their stock was small and very ornate; however, in the grocery section there was an eighty-five-cent earthenware crock with the most ingenious sort of top. Its cork stopper was sealed with a crown of tissue-paper leaves that trailed down over the side of the jar, forming a beautifully intricate border of leaves. Once home, we labored patiently for an hour with a razor blade and cork screw to open the crock without destroying the leaf motif. The fruits of our labor were purely aesthetic, since the contents of the jar was a vegetable relish that had turned rotten.

To counteract that poisonous memory, I keep the little crock for *fresh* bouquets from the vegetable garden. The photograph on page 74 shows it filled with sprigs of red and green cherry tomatoes, garlic greens, and celery tops. I love filling the kitchen with similar arrangements of fruits and garden produce *au natural,* as it were, their leaves and stems intact. Besides the color and gaiety they add to any dark corner or dull countertop, these miniature cornucopias of nature's sweet bounty are a constant reminder of how lucky I am. (Those are not platitudinous words. I often relive the siege of Budapest in 1944, when one egg cost twenty-five dollars and slow starvation was on everyone's face but the enemy's.)

Bouquets of Fresh Edibles

Granted, with fruit trees and a vegetable garden on the place, I do not have to contend with trimmed produce from the supermarket while making one of these edible bouquets. But there are little things a gardenless person can do to achieve the same effect. Instead of taking a bunch of watercress or parsley from your shopping bag and storing it away in the refrigerator, place the bunch of greens in a small pitcher or vase for all to enjoy. You can mix a few flowers with them if you want, simple blossoms like feverfew or daisies. Or put a whole head of Salad Bowl lettuce in a shallow saucer filled with water. Just by itself, the lush green globe is a cheerful centerpiece for an informal dinner. However, when dressed up with strawberries, radishes, cherry or patio tomatoes (they can be raised on apartment terraces or in window boxes), placed in the cradle formed by each lettuce leaf as it branches out from the center stalk, you have an arrangement so full of life it deserves exposure in any room of the house. Small flower blossoms or buds may be substituted for the decorative vegetables.

Be careful, though, that the salad bowl bouquet does not wilt

away, should you wish to enjoy its gastronomic pleasures later. Spray the head with cold water and add ice to the water in the saucer. The arrangement will then remain eating-safe for eight to ten hours, safely within the maximum life expectancy of a good party. On the other hand, watercress or parsley will survive for days as long as they are standing in cold water. If my experience can be taken as a reliable indicator, most hostesses like nothing so much as receiving a floral present that is not florist-bought. A leafy head of lettuce, studded with berries or tiny rose buds, is prized more than two dozen of the latter, open and on eighteen-inch stems. I ought to mention that, if you are the bearer of an edible bouquet, you should plan on assembling the gift in your hostess's home; for the berries have a way of falling from their cradles and dropping by the wayside, when transported from here to there.

Our favorite bit of garden life in the kitchen might very well be called the "boiled beef bouquet." Anyone can make one, whether you are a cook or not. Whenever the supply of frozen dog food leaves room in the garage freezer, I cook large quantities of this great company, or just-us, dish and automatically a vegaquarium starts to grow in the kitchen. Here is how it happens, recipe style.

PLATE 26

Making the Boiled Beef Bouquet

Take one large serving plate that will safely hold a half-inch of water, fill with same. Then, instead of throwing away the tops of the various vegetables that go into a hearty boiled beef, like turnips, celery root, carrots, parsnips, and fresh horseradish (as the relish), cut off the old leaves, leaving only the tiny new shoots and about one-quarter of an inch of vegetable. Place the trimmed and derooted caps in the water-filled serving plate or platter. This assortment of floating islands does not need direct sunlight; yet, in a few days, the stubby shoots will begin their transformation into leafy, green tops. Keep replenishing the dish with water to compensate for normal evaporation. After the first week or ten days, you will start enjoying the formation of what could pass for a miniature Everglade. It encompasses all the childhood fun and excitement of watching an ant colony get established or discovering the first radish shoots of spring. Here is simply a more verdant and fascinating version of the old potato in a glass trick. Caution: One must keep changing the water in a vegaquarium and occasionally wash the roots to prevent rotting.

Solving the Small Flower Holder Problem

The hardest thing to find are miniature vases that do not look cute, holders that are suitable for one large blossom or a nosegay of tiny flowers: lily of the valley, violets, snowdrops, etc. Ceramists seem to lose their sense of proportion as their creations get smaller. Maybe, because of their own diminutive size and veneration for flowers, Orientals excel at fashioning little containers. Over the years, I have collected several Chinese porcelain and enamel bud vases that were just right for working in small scale. The glaze on one of them was too shiny but the bulbous shape intrigued me, so out came a spray can of flat white epoxy paint spray, the kind normally used on tiles. Then, in addition to the small antique American mercury glass holders, previously mentioned, I discovered a few Japanese imitations of this old technique. They are extremely graceful and set off single blooms or several small flowers to great effect. Of course, every store from J.C. Penney to Tiffany stocks the traditional Swedish-made bud vases, those with a tubular stem rising from a ball-like base. Should you get bored with these, as I sometimes do, and want to have a little fun, take a trip to your local liquor store.

My intention is not to lead you astray, I am only suggesting that you may wish to purchase a few of the lilliputian spirit bottles put out by all the major distilleries and wine companies. These come

in dozens of different shapes. None holds more than an ounce and a half or two of liquid and rarely stands higher than three inches. They make ideal containers, when stripped of labels, for the ultimate in diminutive floral presentations, say a single fuchsia blossom or a circumspect camellia. These should not be distributed around the house at random, but touches of levity are surely not out of place on a bathroom shelf, a kitchen counter, or atop that all-American treasure which is just as mind numbing as alcohol —the television set. In our kitchen there is a small built-in desk where most of the household telephoning takes place. To relieve the impersonal monotony of telephonic communications, I often place six or eight of these sample-size liquor bottles on the desk top, fill them with open blossoms, and arrange the group like a small orchestra. Looking at the gay ensemble does away with telephone boredom just as effectively as doodling. The tiny recepta-

Tiny Vases for Solo or Group Display

PLATE 18

Tools and Tricks of the Trade ≥ 77

cles also come in handy when one wants the flower holder to be as unobtrusive as possible, say when blossoms are positioned upon a mirrored tray, where all you want reflected are the underpetals of the flowers.

PLATE 4

Talking about reflections reminds me of a relatively new product on the market that can be used to make reasonably inexpensive flower containers in any size you wish. I am referring to Mylar, the silvery metallic sheeting sold in most hobby shops for about $3.50 a yard. It comes in rolls fifty-four inches wide, does not wrinkle, and can be easily cleaned with a soft cloth and rubbing alcohol. To make your own mirrorlike holder, simply find a size can or leak-proof pot that matches your needs and cover it with a piece of Mylar, using waterproof glue to affix the sheeting to the receptacle, and seal the seam. Recently, manufacturers have come out with a self-patterned Mylar, which has the effect of scrambling into a kaleidoscopic rainbow all the flower or room colors that hit its reflector surface. At the moment, this textured sheeting comes only in six-inch widths and sells for about $1.50 a running foot, so you will probably want to restrict its use to covering small containers. A pretty good idea anyway, since on large areas the jumbling of colors becomes eye-boggling. I frequently cut out coasters from the plain Mylar and place them under containers where I want to mirror the colors of a particular flower arrangement. This system of dressing up an ordinary coffee can or biscuit tin may be followed with those marvelous hand-screened papers utilized by bookbinders for endpapers. Naturally, fabric remnants can serve the same purpose, but remember that in both cases you are not working with a waterproof material and cleaning the covered container will become a problem. Varnishing the paper or cloth will give some, but not permanent, protection.

Masking Holders with Mylar, Fabric, or Paper

Having devoted as much time as I have to the various types and sources of floral containers, I want to be sure—before concluding this section—that I have not left you with a misconception. As vital as the shape and size of a vase or bowl is to the total visual appeal of a flower display, the container is of secondary importance. Nothing must sidetrack the eye from first seeing, and then lingering upon, the flowers themselves. Avoid any receptacle that, because of strong colors or unusual design, fights for the viewer's attention. That is why I favor simple, graceful holders in white or natural shades. When I do pick a vivid red striped jug, let's say, then I use red and white flowers so that they become an integral part of the visual whole. If somebody studies a bouquet of mine and says, "That's a great looking pitcher," I know something went wrong, my priorities got mixed and it is back to the worktable for some stronger blossoms or a less demonstrative pitcher. A good analogy would be that any vase bears the same relationship to the bouquet it contains as a picture frame does to the canvas it holds. Both should compliment and harmonize, but always remain supporting players. I know that the macaroon tin and the plum jam pail would seem to violate this rule, but those are just pleasantries and I am careful not to overdo the joke. As for my pitcher with the hand-painted Iceland poppies diverting one's attention from the real thing, look and decide who won that contest, nature or man.

Visually, Bouquet Must Come First, Container Second

_____

PLATE 11

❦ 6 ❦

Different Bouquets for Different Settings

Each Arrangement Should Bear Its Maker's Signature

The floral compositions in this book represent one person's reaction to the colors, simplicity, and surprises of nature. If you enjoy my way of handling her gifts, then we are attuned to the same stimuli; and a walk together in the garden would generate similar feelings of wonder and satisfaction. Having tried and experimented for so long, perhaps I am better skilled at bringing this excitement into the house in the form of bouquets but, if our reactions parallel, then our endeavors will produce roughly the same results. "Roughly," in this case, has nothing to do with a diminuation of quality. Quite the contrary, it simply recognizes the fact that no two people see things in exactly the same way and, consequently, your floral display should differ from mine. It is this variance that gives a personal imprint to our separate undertakings. Think what a dull world it would be if everyone displayed flowers in the same manner—and, of course, there would be no need for this book.

I have great respect for the ritual and cultural philosophy behind Ikebana, the art of Japanese floral arranging; however, my admiration falls short of honestly liking it. My reservations come from the simple fact that culturally we are closer to the Western world with its freer, more exuberant, and demonstrative ways. One thing Americans are not is inscrutable. The Japanese appreciate geometrically raked areas of sand in their gardens; I love a plush expanse of green lawn. A single inanimate rock may mean as much to them as a towering oak tree does to us. And they carry indoors this same reverence for detail and symbolism. Making one precisely pruned and meticulously balanced magnolia branch the focal point of a room is all very well where a living area is spartanly furnished with the absolute minimum; but that does not happen to be our lifestyle, although getting rid of possessions sometimes seems the easiest alternative to housekeeping. But does that lone branch mirror the flowering profusion, the lush fertility, of the green world around us? More important, where is the radiated warmth that means home? I can understand two precision-placed iris and a sprig of fir being placed on an altar but not upon the fireplace mantel, next to the family clock or photographs of the grandchildren. However, there is one invaluable lesson we can learn from Japanese floral designers: simplicity. That attribute, it can also be called restraint, is probably the hardest one to emulate in making an arrangement. Whether because of our overenthusiasm or lack of discipline, there is always the temptation to add a little more to each bouquet, to end your flower grouping with that "extra touch." Constantly fight the urge, for those last-second additions usually put an end to simplicity. Assuming that you agree, in general, with my nonascetic approach, let's move on to a more generous way of handling flowers.

I keep three major things in mind when confronted with an empty container on "flower days": color, size, and shape; but my

Japanese Versus American Styles in Floral Display

initial thought is where I intend to put the arrangement, since that fact governs all other considerations. Are the flowers to stand in a dark room or one flooded with sunlight? What will be their background—wallpaper, painted walls, or wood paneling? Is the decor of the room modern or period? These are only a few of the questions you will have to ask yourself before deciding what flowers to put where. But such deliberations are necessary only in the beginning. After a brief period of trial and error, one knows instinctively the correct floral combination for a given location. Moreover, you will discover just as quickly the particular spot in a room where a flower arrangement gets the most exposure and makes the greatest impact. A personal example: if there is only time, or enough flowers, to make one bouquet for our living room, it is placed on top of a tall wicker table next to a Thonet lounge. That location is the focal point for all who enter the room because there is a dramatic expanse of embroidery, a tulip-shaped, hanging lamp is the main source of illumination for the area and acts as an unobtrusive spotlight for the floral display, and the height of the table puts a bouquet at eye level. As a matter of fact, when there are no flowers in that spot, the whole room seems empty.

The principal use and purpose of flowers is to brighten one's life emotionally and physically. It is this second attribute that must be taken into account before planning an arrangement. If it is destined for a sunless room or one filled with dark shadows and somber alcoves, then your bouquet should contain lots of white blossoms or, at the very least, light-colored ones. The same theory of floral illumination can be put into practice where the dark patina of antiques is the dominate tone among furnishings. Also, keep in mind that the built-in lighting system provided by white flowers

The Room Site Dictates What Bouquet to Use

Is the Room Dark or Light?

PLATE 1

PLATE 2

PLATE 3

PLATE 4

PLATE 5

PLATE 6

PLATE 7

PLATE 8

PLATE 9

PLATE 10

PLATE 11

PLATE 12

PLATE 13

PLATE 14

PLATE 15

PLATE 16

PLATE 17

PLATE 18

PLATE 19

PLATE 20

PLATE 21

PLATE 22

PLATE 23

PLATE 24

PLATE 25

PLATE 26

PLATE 27

PLATE 28

PLATE 29

PLATE 30

PLATE 31

PLATE 32

PLATE 33

PLATE 34

PLATE 35

PLATE 36

PLATE 37

PLATE 38

PLATE 39

PLATE 40

PLATE 41

PLATE 42

PLATE 43

PLATE 44

PLATE 45

PLATE 46

can be a cheerful aid in the evening. Unless placed near or under a lamp, a white flower catches and reflects the slightest candle-power from distant sources. Often we have come home on a moonlit night and managed, without turning on the lights, to find our way through a darkened room because there were bowls of white marguerites acting as beacons.

There are no color restrictions when you are planning displays for a white, a bright-hued, or sun-filled room. That is probably one reason why I am such an advocate of white, white, and more white in interiors. With that kind of background, anything goes. Brilliant, bold, bright-colored flowers, or, going the other way, you may indulge a preference for subtle pastels, wispy blues, deep dark purples, or quiet mauves. If you only have a single bouquet on hand and want to place the flowers where they will provide the greatest pleasure, cause the most impact, frame them with a white setting.

Do not be put off by the prospect of having to compose a floral arrangement which will go with the wallpaper. Do exactly that—go *Picking* with the paper's pattern assuming, of course, that elephants are *Flowers for* not stampeding across the wall or the design is not a photomontage of the New York City skyline. If the paper or a wall fabric is *Wallpapered* floral, try to make a live reproduction of the pattern; however, *or Paneled* rarely does one have a wide enough selection of cut flowers for *Rooms* that, so pick the dominate blossoms and/or colors in the wall covering and mirror those in your arrangement. The major exception to my rule about going with it occurs when you are dealing with striped papers. With these, I favor working against the grain, so to speak. Vertical lines are best balanced off with low, circular bouquets that create a horizontal plane. Conversely, place tall, thin flower arrnagements or stands of branches in front of papers where the lines, waves, or stripes move from left to right. Finally, when your arrangement is to be close to a nondescript paper or in a wood-paneled room, follow the above rules about painted walls. Dark papers and deep wood finishes are enlivened by having light-colored bouquets in the foreground, but when working in brighter surroundings you can, and should, feature the brilliant shades of your floral palette.

When
Bouquets and
Upholstery
Fabrics
Adjoin

Basically, where prints, chintz, needlework predominate in an area, one can get by with fewer arrangements; but plain uphol-stered pieces, one-shade carpets or rugs and nonpatterned drapes call for a lavish use of flowers and greenery. There are no major problems when planning floral highlights for the latter type of room, since you are dealing with a more or less neutral setting. No element is fighting for attention, nor is one apt to clash with the flowers you wish to introduce. You must be careful, however, when the cushions on a couch, a needlepoint chair seat, or a hand-hooked rug are centers of visual interest in their own right. A very busy or too dominant display of flowers will overpower these deco-rative ingredients, disturbing the harmony of a well-balanced room. There are two ways to treat the problem. The first can be il-lustrated by how that "must" flower position in the living room is handled, the one next to the Thonet chaise. I am always very careful to use blossoms in that spot that match the colors and the scale of the flowers in the needlepointed cushion. As a result, in-stead of the bouquet upstaging the expanse of embroidery, or vice versa, they seem like an adjusted couple—each brings out the best in the other. The second technique is much simpler. Following my theater anology, you let the flowers underplay their role. If you want to put a large basket of flowers on the floor in front of a very vibrant, printed set of drapes, go for simple blossoms in a pure but unobtrusive color that matches an accent in the drape pattern—it could be yellow daisies or white lilacs, for instance. Every good actor knows that understatement is the key to attention and applause.

The same wise rule of avoiding fights whenever it is honorably possible extends to the juxtaposition of flower arrangement and furniture. While they are inseparably joined, with the first perching on the second, there is no reason why one should lord it over the other or why the latter should appear put upon. Generally speaking, when a room is furnished with fine antiques, flowers should be used to add color and life to the rich, dark woods. They also help in *gently* accentuating a particularly fine piece. I stress the word gently because you should avoid large or overly garish floral displays that will call attention away from the very sideboard, Chippendale desk, or highboy that deserves unobstructed study. Talking about well-preserved and highly polished pieces of furniture reminds me of the great pleasure I receive from an unplanned bonus connected with flower arrangements: the ring of fallen petals and pollen, gradually expanding on a rich wood surface, around the base of a flower-filled vase. Don't destroy that charming touch by being too conscientious a housekeeper.

While American, English, and European antiques, from the sixteenth century on, have a built-in warmth, only the most hot-blooded modernist would associate that characteristic with contemporary furnishings and architecture. Modern design, with its accent on severe lines and clean surfaces, its use of so much glass and chrome, can be a chilling experience unless there is an infusion of color to give it warmth. And that is where flowers should come in, masses of them in brilliant, blazing tones. It is almost impossible to overdo the number or variety of floral displays in a modern house. Everything looks well in a stark, purist setting. And if you do not have enough cut flowers, stock the place with green branches, house plants, portable bouquets, trellised vines, even trees. The Scandinavians, pioneers in contemporary design, recognize the visually therapeutic value of nature's gifts. Once, while visiting the Marimekko factory in Helsinki, Finland, I was introduced to an employee who described herself as the company's *kukka tyttö,* or flower girl. This young lady's enviable job was to spend each morning buying bushels of flowers at the open market, down by the harbor, and then to make them up into bouquets, which she distributed throughout the offices, showroom, *and* manufacturing areas of the plant. Long ago, Armi Ratia, founder of Marimekko, decided that contemporary interiors could use the warmth of colorful accessories. Ever since, her fabrics have been a marvelous sea of beautiful, stylized blossoms.

What Decides the Right Size for a Bouquet

The final size of a bouquet is predetermined by its eventual site. Arrangements in a busy area, like a study, where there are many visual distractions, ought to be large enough to match the competition of a cluttered desk, books, pictures, a television set, family mementos, etc. Note, I did not say overpower the surroundings. Under most conditions, you want flowers to stay in balance with the things around them. That goes for small objects, too. Many of us like to place a bowl or vase of flowers next to the photographs of people we love. I know I keep a bouquet of blue cornflowers next to an old picture of my parents in our bedroom. But the stems of those blooms are cut especially short and a small pitcher is used to hold them; for, when looking in that direction, I want the photo to come first, the thought second.

The ideal bouquet is one that does not disturb the general ambience but whose absence is greatly missed. Of course, there are times when you want a flower arrangement to make a big splash, usually for cosmetic reasons. A huge tub filled with flowering dogwood should divert every eye from a worn carpet—except the hostess's. Short of redecorating, the best way to enliven a somber entrance way is with a conspicuous display of white and vibrant colored blossoms. These are just two instances when it is perfectly proper, and helpful, to let a flower arrangement become the center of attention.

So that all the flower arrangements in a given room can be enjoyed separately, try not to station them all at the same eye level. Also, by playing with the heights at which different containers are placed, you make a more interesting and stimulating interior. It is a lesson that can be observed by simply stepping outdoors. When everything in a garden landscape is on the same plane, when the view is not broken up by low and tall flower beds, hedges, staggered trees, and hills, the vista soon loses our attention. Keep that in mind and broaden your horizon, as it were, when choosing locations for floral displays. Start by looking down and utilize empty floor space for baskets and large pitchers, filled with masses of tall flowers, grasses, and branches. Next, move up to the low-lying coffee table or cobbler's bench. At these levels, where one looks down, I favor a low or medium high bouquet, the width of which will depend upon the breadth of the surface and how cluttered it is with other objects like candles, ashtrays, etc. Or, often, where the tabletop is viewed from above, I will make two or three individual bouquets and group the containers together. Then, coming closer to eye level, say for sideboards or wall brackets, you should put together arrangements that look especially rich and full when seen face on or in profile.

Dining room tables would seem to fall in this last category, but

Varying the Eye Level of Where Flowers Are Put

the whole problem of serving around—or talking through—a bushy centerpiece calls for different floral handling. Unless there are servants to keep courses moving and the table clear, I suggest small, individual bouquets at each place setting. They bring the same color and bright life to a dinner party, without the congestion and inconvenience caused by a showy center arrangement, and are thus a lot easier for hostess and guests to cope with. Actually, the small floral offerings are a much more personal touch, too.

PLATE 51 Mantelpieces, pedestals, a tall lectern, an étagère, and the top of cabinets or bureaus are all potential resting places for above eye level flower pieces. When composing these elevated bouquets, be sure to include ferns, ivy runners, soft grasses, and leafy greens that cascade over the lip of the container. That way, the arrangement will reach down and tie in with the room's other floral displays to give the total effect of a floor-to-ceiling garden. Finally, do not overlook the wonderful, escalating display sites provided by steps and staircases, just be sure the flowers and their containers are out of tripping range. Placing them between banister supports and in the corner of broad landings are the safest areas.

Consider the Space Limitations of Where Flowers Stand

A staircase is a rather obvious example of where arrangements must be physically tailored to space and traffic limitations, but there are others that are often overlooked. I have in mind those occasions when a balance must be established between flowers and the space they are to occupy. Say you have decided to brighten up a somber wall in the study by placing a bouquet on the middle shelf of an étagère. Then you should preplan a composition that will look comfortable residing between floors, nothing that hits its head on the shelf above or protrudes so far beyond the sides that it is brushed and disarranged by every passerby. Under such circumstances, put together a grouping of colorful blossoms that

stays within the confines of the boxlike area; but so the arrangement does not seem suspended in midair, allow ferns and other
greenery to gracefully flow over the sides of the étagère. Or, perhaps you would like to dress up an English library step. Then estimate the limits in height and breadth that must be followed to
keep the flowers from appearing top-heavy on their narrow perch.
Careful, though, it is easy to go too far in the other direction. Underplay the size of the bouquet and the piece of furniture will as-
sume massive, ungainly proportions.

The final relationship of size, the one between flowers and container, should be the easiest to manage since, after all, selecting
both the vessel and the blossoms is literally in your hands. Unfortunately, it does not always work out that way. Too many
beginners go on the assumption that if they have filled their favorite pitcher with their favorite blooms, the combination is bound to
look splendid. Not so. The flowers may be too big for the container
or vice versa. You must start the arrangement with one or the
other and, naturally, the flowers should be your first concern. Confronted with a bunch of long-stemmed blossoms, hunt for a receptacle that seems closest to accommodating their height. (Here is
another good reason for pitchers and bowls that are simple in
shape, design, and coloring. They will blend with any room's
decor, should the size of the bouquet require their use.) If you cannot decide which vase will balance out best with the flowers at
hand, be sure to select one that may be a little too small, rather
than a container that is going to prove too tall. After all, it is far
simpler to trim a little off each stem than to fit them with waterproof lifts. Jokes aside, should you ever snip off too much, the
blossoms can be given stilts by gently putting their shortened
stems in paper straws. Flowers with these substitute props will last

PLATE 3

*How to
Choose the
Best Holder
for Each
Bouquet*

almost as long as healthy ones, for they still receive water through capillary attraction. Naturally, the same first aid may be used to elevate normally short-stemmed blossoms, but be careful not to raise them to an artificial-looking level.

Comfortable is as good a word as any to describe the happy state when a proper balance exists between a bouquet and its container. To seem right together, one must not be squeezed into the other. Consider the breadth of your arrangement as well as its height. It is wonderful to see a rich, bright mass of flowers billowing from a container as long as you do not ask yourself, "How did all those blossoms fit into that little vase?" The other extreme, too few blooms for the size of the holder, will create just as ludicrous an effect, only this time the reaction will be, "Those poor, lost flowers."

The next chapter will be devoted solely to the step-by-step mechanics and techniques of creating different kinds of flower arrangements. So that you may devote your full attention to these all-important details, perhaps this is a good time to review the general visual principles that predetermine the finished shape and appearance of every floral display. Shape is all a matter of proportion, one of those innate instincts that, unfortunately, cannot be learned from any book in a do-it-yourself library; but it is a sense that may be developed through trial and error. Therefore, by exploring in advance some of the most common errors, we ought to be able to greatly reduce the chances of your having to commit them. Beginners, putting together an arrangement, should pause now and then to survey the work in progress. If during these moments of inspection, any of the following words come to mind, you will know you have to stop and do some rearranging. The stoplights are: top-heavy, lopsided, crowded, skimpy. Taking these faults one by one, here are ways to rectify them.

The Most Common Mistakes in Flower Arranging

Top-heavy: Chances are you started your bouquet with flowers that were relatively the same height and failed to trim their stems to varying lengths. Consequently, most of the blossoms are standing head to head at the top of the arrangement. As a group, they probably resemble a flat-crowned mushroom. Flowers in a garden do not reach one level and then stop growing on command, so why regiment them in a bouquet? Take daisies as an example. Marquerites are cut from a bush that is round as a ball, with blossoms on the top, sides, and down near the ground. Achieve this allover lushness with cut flowers by staggering their lengths, be they daisies, mums, or marigolds.

When working with flowers that are relatively uniform in height and erect in stature, things like gladiolus, daffodils, and tulips, there are several ways to avoid a bunched-at-the-top look. I am for cutting some of them down to irregular lengths for use in a vase or pitcher, but I know this will be considered needless slaughter by many. One alternative to my suggested crime would be to round out the gap between blossom level and container top with softer blossoms of another specie or with greens. The next possibility is to place, say, daffodils in a very wide-mouthed bowl and, with the help of Oasis, stand them up in random-spaced clumps, leaves and all, thus matching their natural growing habit. Remember, earlier in the book, we mentioned camouflaging the soil around "instant bouquets" with a layer of sphagnum moss? Well, cover the block or blocks of Oasis, which are holding the tulips, in the same manner. For this to work, your bowl must be a shallow one. Oasis is only three inches high and you want the moss to be even with the lip of the bowl. The sphagnum will absorb water until it is the consistency of a soaked sponge. At this point, you can plant it with a very short-stemmed flower, say pansies, violets, or Johnny-jump-ups. There will be no blanks in the underpinnings of your arrangement now.

Lopsided: This defect usually stems from fixing flowers too hastily or by failing to construct the arrangement flower by flower, which are really one and the same reasons. Do not work with flowers if you are in a rush, as we all are a great deal of the time. It is a pursuit requiring patience and the leisure to reflect. Besides, all the rewards of working with nature's gifts are lost when we are under the pressure of other priorities. That is why I suggest that if you are making floral arrangements for a party, do them the day or night before.

I assure you, I am not in the habit of making work for myself, but there is no way to produce an arrangement of which you are proud when its merits can only be seen from a certain angle. The majority of floral displays are placed where people have a 360-degree view of them or else they are against a wall or in a corner with two or three sides exposed. Only when a bouquet rests in a niche or is closely flanked, perhaps by books, can you be sure of always putting its best face forward. Naturally, no matter how thorough you are, one side of an arrangement will look better than the others. It is this good angle that I always point toward the entrance of the room, so that when visitors enter, each bouquet seems to be waiting for them, anxious to say hello. Nevertheless, the other three views must be almost as presentable.

Concern over lopsidedness should not be confused with worrying about whether an arrangement is symmetrical. There is no need for the latter. The perfectly balanced, be it floral or human, grows tiresome. The eye as well as the mind feasts upon irregularities. In both cases, one only becomes concerned when the imperfection drags down everything connected with it. There is charm and a natural—no getting away from that adjective when talking about the ways of nature—incongruity to a lone rose that droops casually sideways while its companions play out their role of upright, proud flowers. Or what about a branch of mimosa spilling over one side of a vase and dripping downward—like the pregnant-heavy limbs of the acacia tree when in golden full bloom—until their blossoms dust the tabletop with pollen? Those are the non-symmetrical elements, planned or accidental, that give a flower grouping character and personality. The trick is not to overdo these touches or your work will appear contrived and out of kilter. When the periphery of a bouquet is disturbingly jagged or contains a grouping of flowers that draws attention away from the main body of the arrangement, inventiveness has become self-defeating. As in a well-executed painting or watercolor, every floral display should have a focal point, a spot the eye continually returns to; however, the focal point must not be so predominant that one is distracted from taking in the whole of which it is a small part.

Crowded: When expressing a preference for arrangements where flowers are massed together, I was not talking about sheer numbers. I like a rich, full sampling of nature, but that effect can be achieved without packing the blossoms petal to petal. In fact, when the latter takes place, you fail to see the faces for the crowd and your senses get caught in the crush, unable to discern the beautiful from the ordinary. Sometimes it is not numbers alone that creates this oppressive feeling of mass. An indiscriminate mixture of many different kinds of flowers in different colors will produce the same perplexing results. The eye is asked to absorb too much. It gives up, or simply registers confusion.

Both crowding and/or busyness may be eliminated from an arrangement by judiciously weeding out the excesses and using them in a companion bouquet. Far simpler, though, is to use restraint from the very beginning, taking care that as you put in each flower, it will occupy a space of its own. As for the blinding rainbow kind of flower arrangement, we would never be subjected to their glare if people would content themselves with discovering, and using, the multitude of different hues within one color family and then mixing those with one, at the most two, primary colors. But, more about that when we come to the section on color.

Skimpy: Anemic-looking flower displays usually have nothing to do with an absence of flowers. More likely, improper structuring of the floral elements at hand is to blame. Unless you are a magician, a beautiful bouquet just doesn't spring into being. A little planning is involved.

Before starting, fix in your mind a rough picture of how you would like the finished arrangement to turn out. Which color or flower do you want to predominate? Is it to have a quiet, romantic feeling or are you after something bursting with gaiety? In connection with achieving a certain mood, keep in mind that the flowers used will have much of the say. Rust-colored snapdragons can be lovely but they are hardly my idea of a proper prelude to romance and it is rather hard to imagine lilies, hybrid or calla, being featured in a joyous bouquet of celebration. So, having decided the direction you wish to take, begin structuring toward that goal, being sure to use the appropriate floral ingredients. However, everybody runs out of flowers at one time or another and something has to be done to fill gaps or flesh out the sides of a bouquet. That is when you reach for greens. My way is to try and use them as another color in the arrangement, not as bandaids to be stuck here and there, covering problem areas.

And I am very selective about the greens that I do use. Unfortunately, many of my favorite flowers are wedded to unattractive leaves—cosmos, the gloriosa daisy, to name two. When working with these flowers and others similarly afflicted, I always strip them down to the bare stem. Then if there are no beautifully leafed flowers in the arrangement, I will borrow stand-ins from better-endowed plants. Nasturtium, violet, and ivy greens are perfect for encircling small blossoms. But if there is nothing at hand for the larger arrangements, do not hesitate to use small-leafed branches, like those from a forsythia bush when it has finished blooming, or celery and carrot tops, dill gone to seed, and stalks of mint. Nor should you treat with disdain the various wild grasses and common weeds. I frequently use long shafts of rye and crab grass to soften, break up, or fill out a floral grouping. As a matter of fact, a clump of crab grass all by itself in a container makes for a fresh

Borrowing Leaves from One Flower to Enhance Another

Different Bouquets for Different Settings ❧ 95

and amusing display, one which is not cute. To do anything "cute" with nature's gifts takes top spot on my list of flower-arranging sins. Well, I guess I can think of something worse, but it is too funny to be taken seriously. I once saw—and smelled—a bouquet that a woman had just sprayed with floral-scented perfume.

Extending the Indoor Display Life of Bulbs

Before leaving the subject of greens, let me go back a moment to those portable bouquets for a switch on my practice of taking leaves from one plant to exhibit with the flowers of another. Forcing bulbs—tulips, daffodil, hyacinth, etc.—in and for the house, certainly fits the category of instant flower displays; but these plants have a sad drawback. The flowers die very quickly. However, and here comes the happy part, their leaves live on, firm and green, for weeks. I capitalize on the continued presence of the latter by sticking a fresh-cut flower in the place of the dearly departed. You don't even have to match flower to leaf but doing so makes the trick less easy to detect. If the soil around the surviving plant is kept soaked to sustain the Lazaruslike flower, you can count on the subterfuge lasting for several days, certainly time enough to get through a weekend of entertaining or, far more important, to help you privately survive an attack of the midwinter blues. And you can keep adding fresh flowers for weeks.

❦ 7 ❦

Putting It All Together

Your principal concern when making an arrangement is being sure that you are working with very fresh flowers and foliage. Anything less shortens the fruits of your labors. The problem is a relatively simple one for those who grow their own. Flowers store life-sustaining nutrients during the night, which are gradually used up in the daylight hours. Consequently, it is the early bird who gathers the freshest, strongest blossoms. To be doubly sure that you get them into the house in the same top condition on overly hot or sunny days, take a pail of warm water into the garden with you to temporarily store just-picked blossoms. Such a precautionary measure is not necessary on cool or overcast days. Of course, gathering flowers after sundown and keeping them in a cold, dark place—cellar, garage, refrigerator—for use the next day is another procedure to avoid the debilitating effects of harvesting in sunshine.

When buying at a florist shop, there are numerous ways to check on the freshness of your purchase. First look at the leaves. They should be green and firm, free of curled edges. Shake multi-petal blossoms, like delphiniums, to see that none shed. You

How to Find,

and Keep,

Flowers Fresh

should be able to cleanly snap off the ends of strong-stemmed flowers, such as chrysanthemums, stocks, and snapdragons. If it requires twisting to break them, they are not in top condition. Be equally skeptical of blooms where the petals are thin or almost transparent. Whenever possible, try to find flowers that are in their bud, or just opening, stage. Naturally, that won't work when you are shopping for a bouquet that has to be in full bloom for a spur-of-the-moment party. But should you need fully opened flowers and you are a regular customer of an honest florist, the chances are you will find him willing to sell these less-than-pristine specimens at a reduced price. Perhaps because roses are among the easiest flowers to judge for freshness, unscrupulous vendors are given to subterfuge. Their most common trick is to take off the outer, wilted petals of opened blossoms, leaving what looks like a tight, fresh head on the stem. You can detect such cheating by closely inspecting the base of the rose for petal scars. Also, press the blossom between your thumb and index finger to be sure that it is full and firm. Under no circumstances should you purchase flowers whose stems or buds have been wired, no matter what excuse the florist gives.

Water: For Storage, Vases, and Rejuvenating

Atop my worktable and on the floor surrounding it, buckets and pails of cold and warm water are lined up to receive the cut flowers as soon as they are brought in from the garden. Use the tepid water for buds, if you want them to open in a hurry. Naturally, the same routine may be followed to awaken unopened blossoms in the house. Now, many readers will be working with flowers ordered from a florist or received as a gift, and these frequently wilt in transit. Like a good wine, flowers do not travel very well and when they arrive at their new destination they need a drink—and fast. In fact, sticking the weary, thirsty flowers in cold water sometimes is not enough to revive them. In those instances, submerge the entire bouquet in a sink full of warm water, snip a half-inch off of each stem—cutting under water—and let them remain totally immersed for about twenty more minutes.

I know that most everyone advises changing the water in flower arrangements each day. If you have only a precious few blossoms for the house, do so by all means to prolong the bouquet's life. But home gardeners, with a backup supply of fresh substitutes on hand, need not be so attentive. I rarely make the daily change, although I do keep adding fresh water, or leftover ice cubes, to containers to make up for the rapid evaporation that takes place indoors. This is doubly important in the winter when windows are shut and a house is being heated. Since cut flowers are deprived of the rejuvenating effect of dew and rainfall, try to mist them once or twice a day with one of those fine sprayers, normally sold for house plant culture. This, too, will prevent blooms and leaves from drying out.

When you are taking flowers to a party, save your hostess from having to go through the underwater resuscitation process by delivering your gift super fresh. This can be done by preparing the bouquet at the very last minute. Wrap the stems in wet paper towels and insert them in a plastic bag. Put a couple of ice cubes inside the protective wrapping so that the blanket of towels does not dry out. Then cinch the plastic bag around the sheaf of stems with rubber bands, or a length of Twist'ems, to reduce evaporation and prevent spillage.

Neither constant water changes, ice cubes, spraying, nor compensating refills will extend the life of cut flowers unless you keep every holder immaculately free of the algae and rotting leaves that settle on the bottom and sides of vases, pitchers, and bowls. While adding several drops of household bleach (Clorox, Purex, etc.) to the water of a finished arrangement will help in that direction, it is imperative that other steps be taken to maintain sanitary containers. After each use, scrub away all deposits with a strong detergent. When the holders are badly stained, let them soak overnight in a solution of soapy water and a little ammonia. You will have far less residue to cope with, if you always make a practice of stripping every leaf from those parts of the stems that are below the waterline.

Finally, as long as we are talking about the optimum preservation of a cut flower's blooming life, I should mention that small number that close at night. I learned about these the hard way. About fifteen years ago, for the first party in our new home, I thought it appropriate to gather several small bouquets of California poppies and another wild flower, yellow oxalis. The dinner was a great success, although the symbolism of my floral arrangements was a total flop—I had chosen two plants whose blossoms close at night. Since that show of ignorance, I have learned how to keep these early sleepers awake in the presence of company. Now I pick them before their petals open in the morning, place them in a container of cold water, and store the two in the refrigerator. Unscrew the light bulb in the latter to maintain the ruse of total darkness until evening and the arrival of your guests. At that point, place them on the dinner table where they will think the artificial light is daybreak and their blossoms unfold. Day lilies can be fooled in the same way, but they require very strong illumination to open and

First, Separate Your Flowers by Color

who wants to eat with all the lights turned on high.

Just as I pick flowers by color and size, so too is my harvest separated in water-filled containers within arm's length of the work-table. I use two- and five-pound tins to store the shorter cuttings, while several five-gallon cans, cadged from departing house painters, stand on the floor nearby to hold the taller flowers and branches, like Queen Ann's lace and forsythia. Then there is usually a pail filled with ferns, leaves, and other greenery. After a morning's pickings have been thus sequestered according to color, my arranging area has the look of a giant palette. And when the exciting moment comes to start creating with flowers, I use it exactly as a still-life painter would, reaching for a particular yellow to mix with oranges, taking a stalk or two of blue forget-me-nots to highlight a spray of white sweet peas, or selecting some lemon leaves to fill in a background with green. In one sense, my live palette is far superior to any artist's, for the pure, true colors that come from nature are not to be squeezed from any tube.

I was clearly born too late. According to the marvelous old movies of the Thirties—I watch them avidly to lessen the monotony of embroidery—flower arranging was a cinch in those days. It seems that all Katharine Hepburn or Joan Fontaine had to do was bounce in from the garden with fresh-cut flowers in their arms and drop the bunch into the nearest empty vase. Presto: a perfectly arranged bouquet. There wasn't even the need to go fetch water. I guess parlor maids kept all the containers filled, knowing how quickly their mistresses liked to brighten up a piano top or a table in the front hall. It's back to reality, I'm sorry to say; for, unless you are under contract to Metro-Goldwyn-Mayer, the only way to compose a beautiful floral display is one flower at a time. Just as a mason has to build a wall brick by brick, a bouquet is made flower by flower. The analogy can be carried a few steps farther. Masons start their construction at the bottom; so should you. And both endeavors require a solid foundation.

Depending on the size of your arrangement and the type of container selected, there are four commonly used underpinnings for floral displays.

Arrangements Must Be Put Together Flower by Flower

Chicken wire, small gauge and medium weight, should be employed as the foundation for tall arrangements of heavy-headed blossoms: dahlias, chrysanthemums, etc. Using wire cutters or pliers—not your pruning shears, they'll knick—cut a piece of mesh that is a little bigger in circumference than the base of your container. Roll over the edges of the wire until it can be wedged into place at the bottom of the vase or bowl. Should the flowers be extra tall or top-heavy, make a similar mesh holder to insert at the top of the container. There will be no need for the second one if you are using a narrow-necked pitcher. Mesh holders in glass vases need camouflaging. Hide them with sphagnum moss or leaves that do not rot in water, like ivy or rhododendron.

Oasis, Florapack, or the other porous synthetics sold in craft and florist shops should be used to anchor lightweight, thin-stemmed flowers in bowls and baskets. It usually comes in brick form and may be cut with a knife to fit the shape of a small container or several blocks can be placed side by side to fill up the bottom of larger ones. Initially, Oasis floats, so, prior to use, soak the substance in water until it is thoroughly saturated. Woody, thin stems will slip into the sodden block quite easily, but for more delicate or pulpy ones, make their entrance easier by poking holes with an awl or ice pick.

Metal-pronged holders come in various sizes, are a must for those interested in making modern, or Japanese-inspired, arrangements, those that utilize very shallow containers. One normally trims stems at an oblique angle to increase water intake, but with these holders you will often find it necessary to cut closer to a straight horizontal so the end can stick securely on the metal needles. Should you have trouble poking a tough branch into one of these holders, mash its end a little with a few blows of a hammer.

The bad habit the metal devices have of slipping this way and that can be curbed by anchoring the holder with florist clay, a form of plasticine. However, be sure you adhere holder to container bottom before adding water or the fixative will not stick.

Polished stones, agates, pebbles, and white gravel are some of the natural weights often employed to hold flowers in their proper place. Many find the first two particularly attractive solutions when using clear glass vases or bowls. With very heavy branches or simply tall ones, like pussywillow, forsythia, and, of course, sunflowers, you will need extra heavy weights, not only to keep the arrangement from shifting about but to prevent the container from tipping over. I have often used rocks, even bricks, at the bottom of a favorite, tall, urn-shaped basket to counterbalance cascading sprays of leaves and flowering branches.

Having given the traditional ways of holding and bracing flowers in an arrangement, let me emphasize that, whenever possible, I prefer not to use these artificial props. Over dependence on them leads to the one thing I try most to avoid in bouquets—a stiff, artificial, overly structured look. Ideally, I want my flowers to appear as they do in nature, like a herbaceous garden border where they are always close together, competing for light and space, seemingly wanting to outdo each other when it comes to color and size. To capture this effect, and reduce my dependence on store-bought holders, I use "natural fillers." I have coined the phrase in order to designate those multibranched flowers that grow in clumps. The best of them, for arranging purposes, are feverfew, Queen Ann's lace, forget-me-nots, and marguerites. Both visually and structurally, they are ideal ingredients for a mixed bouquet. Here is how to use these holder substitutes.

Divide your choice of filler flower into two, roughly equal

Letting Flowers Serve As Their Own Holders

bunches, cutting the stems of one shorter than the other. Then, using a broad-mouthed bowl or a wide-necked pitcher, fill the orifice with the batch of smaller fillers, crisscrossing their stems at the bottom of the container. When done correctly, you will have formed a tangled anchor of interwoven stems, a live version of the chicken-wire holder. The upper bushiness of the fillers, pressing against each other, keeps the underwater structure from coming apart. Now, start sticking your different flowers into the filler framework, leaving for the last the blossoms you wish to be dominant. Some should go in so that you only see them in profile, of others there should be a three-quarter view; but position most of them facing you, for that is the viewpoint from which the bouquet will eventually be observed. You are not distorting nature's ways with this face-front positioning, since, in a way, that is really what flowers do outdoors—always turning their heads in one direction, trying to get the sun's attention. Get out your clippers and play with the height of each new addition to the arrangement. That way, you will be capturing a little more of the look of a mixed garden, where flowers range in height from dwarf to extra tall. Do not forget to cut stems at a sharp angle, at least forty-five degrees, to aid water intake. Where you need to hold some flowers in position, use your longer-stemmed fillers trimmed to staggered elevations. The latter can also be inserted where gaps appear in the bouquet. Finally, fill in the back of the arrangement with the least important or not perfect blossoms. Should you run out of flowers all together, use greens. Just don't leave it with bare flanks. Small flowering fruit cuttings and twig-size greens make equally fine natural fillers.

Some flowers are simpler to work with than others. So, if you are new to the pleasures of flower arranging, it might be wise and a great deal more fun to begin with the "easy flowers." I call them

that because stiff-stemmed blossoms with simple shapes call for a minimum of embellishing in a bouquet. The following seem able to stand on their own, both literally and figuratively:

iris	anemones
chrysanthemums	marigolds
(includes daisies)	zinnias
geraniums	delphiniums
primroses	gladiolus
larkspur	stocks
snapdragons	cattail
foxglove	

Then there are all the leafy, stiff branches that are often floral displays in themselves. They, too, are easy to arrange, last a long time, and, when trimmed to different heights, provide another natural framework and anchor for keeping more difficult flora in place. Incidentally, do not be afraid of cutting up one large and overly full branch into several more easily usable ones. However, avoid clipping the main branch in half to get two display sprays, since the lower section will be way out of proportion with the thinner top. What you do do, though, is simply prune off the side shoots for extra fillers. The most readily available of these easy helpers are:

dogwood	holly
forsythia	pine
pussywillow	boxwood
lilacs	flowering fruits
snowballs	citrus leaves
camellia	oleander
firethorn	heather

Last, but probably first in the hearts of all beginning flower arrangers is that master problem solver—the fern, particularly members of the asparagus family. Aside from being one of the best of the natural fillers, they can serve to collar a small bouquet with a sheath of delicate green, fill out the base of a larger one, and make up for a shortage of blossoms in most any floral display. The fact is that ferns are so adaptable, I sometimes think they are overused when other, less common greens would lend more originality and flair to an arrangement.

A Tip Sheet for Healthier, Prettier Bouquets

The more you work and create with flowers, the longer becomes your list of individual do's and don'ts. Through trial and error, each person develops his own little arranging habits. Many of these variations on the basic techniques can be observed in the look and style of a bouquet; others may be hidden, but they aid in prolonging the life span and health of an arrangement. Until a pattern has been established that works best for you, my tip sheet may be helpful. Some of the following items have been mentioned in other sections of this book, but I think they are important enough to warrant repeating.

(1) When picking or buying flowers or leaves, always cut or purchase ones with stems longer than you need. This is especially important with branches.

(2) Whenever possible, try to combine in a bouquet both the buds and open blossoms of the flowers used.

(3) Either in the garden or at the florist, select some flowers with twisted and bent stems. Without irregularity, beauty is dull.

(4) To salvage flowers with broken or drooping stems, gently insert a wet pipe cleaner into the damaged section.

(5) Snip a little off the tops of heavy branches and sprays of berries to reduce their top-heaviness.

(6) *Always* select and use roses with tightly closed buds. And don't overlook the special charm and long-lasting qualities of single roses.

(7) Zinnias and dahlias, on the other hand, should be picked or purchased when in full bloom. They cannot be forced from bud to blossom stage, once cut.

(8) De-spire the spikey flowers and they have an entirely different feeling. I do this often with delphiniums and would try the same with gladiolus, if I liked them more. PLATE 35

(9) Many people seem to object to the way delphiniums keep dropping their petals. I do not consider their fallout a mess; but for those who do, strip wilting flowers from the base of the stalk and trim the stem. Result: a shorter delphinium with blossoms about to open.

(10) Dip milky or pulpy stems (like those of poppies) in boiling

water to clear the channels for water absorption. Singeing the flower end over a gas burner or with a candle will have the same effect.

(11) To rejuvenate faded or overly opened roses and peonies, wrap them completely in newspaper, twisting shut both ends of the covering. Then place the package in a sink or tub, covering it with an inch of warm water, and allow to soak for several hours.

(12) So that they may better absorb water, break up the ends of roses with several taps of a hammer. Follow the same procedure with other woody stems.

(13) Each time you change water in a container, remove all decaying leaves and retrim stem ends at a slant. Let those arrangements, too difficult to change, stand in a sink under slowly running cold water.

(14) Never place cut flowers near a heat vent. If your house is full of floral arrangements, set the thermostat as low as possible and be sure to add water and/or ice cubes to containers to make up for evaporation loss. Also, under hot and dry conditions, or just prior to a party, spray blossoms and foliage with cold water.

(15) Until you know what type of bouquets go best where—it takes time and practice to judge what is right for a house—I find it helpful to carry container and prepared flowers to a possible site and make the arrangement there. In that way, changes can be made on the spot to conform with the final setting.

The Five Basic Floral Shapes and How to Make Them

While no two bouquets ever look precisely alike because of their varied floral content, actually all flower arrangements may be broken down geometrically into five basic shapes. Taking them one by one, here is how they look and where they look their best. *Round:* The all-purpose shape, constructed to be seen from every angle; can be placed anywhere it will physically fit in a room. *Vertical:*

These large bouquets require a good deal of room. When put on, or near, large pieces of furniture, they will help minimize the heaviness of the latter. The ideal shape for arrangements that are to stand on the floor. *Triangle:* Actually, there are two kinds of these, symmetrical ones and those where one side is longer than the other. The first is not my favorite because they appear so formal and evenly structured, which of course they are. However, these go well in the center of a mantelpiece, on a console or sideboard, any place where the objects to the right and left of the bouquet are in balance. Asymmetrical flower pieces help to break up the monotony of straight lines. Consequently, they should be stationed at the end of long benches, coffee tables, and buffets, or on one side of the mantel. *Fan:* Being relatively two-dimensional, with most flowers facing front, these arrangements are perfect for placement on surfaces that do not have too much depth: narrow shelves or tables close to a wall, up against room dividers, in corners and niches. *Sphere:* This is a pincushionlike bouquet, best appreciated when seen from above; therefore, they are perfect for coffee tables and benches. But, if you use a low container and restrict the height of the floral sphere, such a shape will work equally well on a dinner table.

Now, let's move on to the actual mechanics of making the five different-shaped arrangements.

Round: This is my favorite. It incorporates all the irregularity and lushness of a garden in full bloom. Lots of flowers are called for and they are packed together. They work well in large-necked pitchers, deep bowls, goblets. Although I very rarely find it necessary, you may wish to place chicken wire in the mouth of the container. I start by inserting several leafy branches and short greens. The first will give body to the bouquet and, incidentally, reduce the number of flowers you will have to use; while the second is there to cover the mesh. Small flowers will eventually be placed around the

rim and these may make the camouflaging greens unnecessary. If so, you may choose to remove them when the arrangement is completed. Next, I add large flowers (roses, peonies, zinnias, etc.) in clusters of three or four to provide strong splashes of color. These should be long-stemmed, so that they crisscross on the bottom of the vase or bowl, allowing the blossoms to fall in all directions. Then insert some natural fillers, ones with long, thin stems and delicate flowers, like feverfew, Korean chrysanthemums, or daisies. Flowering branches may be substituted for, or used to supplement, the last. The final step is to fill in empty spaces with shorter stemmed flowers and place small blossoms around the edge of the container.

The round shape may also be adapted to feature one type of flower and that is just what I do when a particular variety comes PLATE 15 into bloom in the garden, say zinnias. Cut the flowers in staggered lengths before placing them in the container and add wild grasses or other delicate greens to soften the allover appearance. Also, you will find that the insertion of *naturally* bent-over blossoms, cascading branches, dangling greens, etc., give a light and less formal air to any combination in the round framework.

Vertical: These arrangements go in tall containers: pitchers, bottles, jugs, and cylinders. Personally, I avoid the last, finding that they bunch flowers together and look too similar to the bouquets they hold. Verticals, require long-stemmed flowers such as foxglove (digitalis), and bearded iris and/or branches in bloom: forsythia, mimosa, pussywillow, etc. When selecting the ingredients for this type of display, they should be three times the height of the container. Of course, you will subsequently trim some of the flowers and branches to graduated lengths. Be sure, however, that they all touch the bottom of the container to avoid having the arrangement topple over. You can finish up with smaller, full-faced flowers to play thin and tall against fat and round. To counteract the feeling of stiff formality that this shape  sometimes generates, include crooked branches, wispy grasses, or some off-balance leaves.

If you have no tall containers, the same vertical effect can be achieved using some shallow bowl or disk, but Oasis or metal-pronged holders will have to be utilized to support the tall flowers in the arrangement. Follow the same principle as when constructing the larger version of a vertical display; but use lighter weight flowers, say gerberas, daffodils, agapanthus, roses, tulips, or narcissus. While it is good to place two or three of the same flower together for a bold color accent, do not crowd all the blossoms in one area or you will end up with a confined, cylinder shape.

Triangle: The symmetrical version looks well in trumpet-shaped vases, urns, or wide-mouthed pitchers. You will need chicken-wire anchoring here, to maintain the precise, stylized form. Start by placing one or two spire type blossoms in the center, and slightly to the rear, of the container. These, the tallest components of the bouquet, should be about twice the height of the container se-

lected. Then take two equal length flowers, let's say they are delphiniums, and fan them out to the right and to the left of the center spire along the base of the bouquet. Now, a line connecting the tip of the center flower and the side delphiniums gives you the triangular outline into which all the other flowers must fall. To keep this pyramidlike arrangement even, all stems must radiate from the same point at the base and each floral addition to the right of the center spire must be balanced off on the left by a flower of similar type and length. If you want to feature the color and size of one particular flower, a number of them should be placed in the center of the triangle, facing front. I usually use this shape only when there is a limited supply of flowers—I pad with leaves and greenery—or when I want a bouquet to cascade from a high piece of furniture. In the latter case, you simply extend the length of the flowers forming the base of the triangle until they hang down below the bottom of the container.

The asymmetrical shape is much more fun to make and, personally, I feel the finished arrangement has greater excitement and freedom than its formal, even-sided relation. Just start by placing your tallest flowers off center. If you began with these on the left, then your next step is to build downward with most of your flowers going to the right. When you get to that corner of the triangle, keep right on adding blooms. This has the effect of making one side of the arrangement much lower than the other. In fact, depending on the length of flowers inserted, the right-hand corner

of the bouquet will touch the tabletop or dangle over its edge. Since, by the nature of their name, asymmetrical displays are uneven, there is no need to balance right and left with the same type and quantity of blooms; however, a certain similarity should prevail to give the shape cohesion and solidity. A note of caution: triangles, even or uneven, are probably the most difficult shapes to  ably the most difficult shapes to execute well, so I would not advise neophytes to begin with these. Sometimes I even wonder if they are worth all the work involved.

Fan: They spread out best when placed in low, open-necked bowls or rectangular containers. While this is probably the easiest

to construct of the five shapes, it requires a wire mesh holder, for the flowers used are reasonably tall and they must all arise from a low-sided container. Also, each stem is placed as close to the central one as possible. The latter is the tallest and placed in position  first. Then, working to right and left, fill in the other spokes of the fan, cutting each a little shorter than its predecessor. Fill in gaps in the front of the fan but do not bring the blossoms down to the lip of the container. Like the wooden stays of an actual fan, the bare stems should be seen. Stiff, straight-stemmed flowers—iris, chrysanthemums, and the like—are ideal for this shape, but tulips, roses, anything with a sturdy, clean stalk will fit this type arrangement. To achieve an airy, delicate feeling, leave space between the blossoms and set the bouquet against a contrasting background. Conversely, should you wish a dramatic eye-catcher or something that will brighten a dark corner, pack the flowers in the fan as close together as possible.

Sphere: To faithfully reproduce the moundlike appearance of this arrangement, you must use a relatively low bowl, one having a wider mouth than base. Now, there are those who advocate first

building up another sphere of Oasis within the container and sticking each flower into such a pincushion. I find that a great deal of trouble, especially since I often use the shape for weak-stemmed flowers (pansies, violets, nasturtiums) that cannot be pushed into

Oasis unless a separate hole is punched for each blossom. A very small mesh wire holder is more efficient under those circumstances. While I personally prefer only using the sphere for flowers with "faces," it is adaptable to all round blossoms, like small dahlias, zinnias, ranunculus, and marigolds. But it is not a good shape for heavy, large blooms. Of course, one can mix the types of flowers in this sort of arrangement, but to do so lessens the visual impact for me and so I work with only one.

You start a sphere bouquet by placing a row of blossoms, cheek to cheek, around the lip of the container, faces looking straight ahead. With each ensuing circle of flowers, the heads should be turned a little more toward the zenith. Try to interweave the stems with the wire for a firmer hold, although each concentric circle will be easier to place, since the blooms brace themselves against the row below. Naturally, in as much as you are constructing a floral dome, the closer a flower is to the top, the longer its stem will have to be. When you have laid in the last, tiny circle of flowers, the bouquet will look a little like those Easter bonnets that white-haired, pink-cheeked ladies love to wear each spring. If the finished arrangement strikes you as overly even—or too much like a hat—you can make it more irregular by substituting buds for some of the flower faces or by simply pulling out a few of the blossoms so that they are not flush with their neighbors.

8

A Bouquet of Colors

Millions upon millions of words have been written about the theory and principles of color; but, when everything has been said on the subject, it all comes down to you. Color, like beauty, is in the eye of the beholder. However, there is a catch. The National Bureau of Standards recognizes 267 different colors and shades. Now that is an awesome rainbow to behold. No wonder so many are afraid or too bewildered to make color choices and decisions. There really is no need, though, to let the uncommon inhibit you; for, like any other field of knowledge, color can be mastered through education and doing. And flower lovers are lucky, since the best teacher and workshop in color is Nature itself. You may feel apprehensive about assembling the components for your first few arrangements—it is rather like agonizing over what-shall-I-wear; but, please believe me, so much will be learned from those initial efforts about what color combinations are *right for you* and for *your home* that assembling flower groupings will eventually become an instinctive act. The material in this chapter is meant to get you through the trial and error period.

Even in the face of 267 choices, all of us grow up with certain color favorites. Of course, they may change—and probably will—with age and experience; but that is why, for security's sake, I originally suggested planting or purchasing only flowers in the shades you feel comfortable with. That way, color becomes far less of a problem when putting together a floral arrangement. However, it must be remembered that although there are few, if any, color clashes in nature's green arena, once you separate flowers from their brethren and background and make them stand face to face in a pitcher, some chromatic fights are bound to break out. Take orange bird-of-paradise—I know I don't want to—standing behind a bed of powder blue forget-me-nots. In the wide reaches of the garden, such an odd combination is neutralized; but bringing the two into the house for use in a dining room centerpiece is like serving a sidedish of marinated herring with a cheese souffle. Since there will always be those who consider fish and cheese a marvelous treat, there is no point entering into an endless debate about what is good taste in food—or color. Besides, I can only write with authority about the colors and color combinations that please me most and seem to work best in my floral arrangements.

The Colors That Are Right for You Are the Ones to Use

As you surely have gathered by now, I love pure, bright colors the most. They bring excitement and warmth to a room, spreading hope and joy on the bleakest of days, on the saddest occasions. You will find, also, that color seems to psychologically change physical conditions. For example, to make our cool blue bedroom even cooler, it is filled with all the blue flowers and green ferns I can lay my hands on. In winter, along with the thermostat in that room, hot-hued flowers are turned on. And then there are aesthetic considerations to keep in mind when matching bouquets to your environment. If you have a house like ours, which is basically white,

Coloring Bouquets to Help Your Environment

use as many yellow, red, and blue flowers as possible. And loads of white. You can still use the same primary colors in a darker house, but concentrate on their lighter shades. No need to worry about blue flowers being too subdued for somber settings, since most of the blues in nature are either on the very light side or have a lot of violet in them. Stay away, though, from bouquets that are heavy in magenta and rose colors. You'll get them anyway, without even trying, for this is the one shade that seems to surface, sooner or later, in almost every flower family.

Arrangements
Composed of
Monochromes

One can put a great deal of color into a bouquet without resorting to a lot of different colors. What I am talking about is a monochromatic arrangement, one that exploits the endless tints, hues, and shades in a single primary color. Handling flowers this way is virtually foolproof, should you have doubts about your color sense. If nature can put a dozen different reds in the face of one blossom, then you can use the same varied tones when selecting her flowers for the house. The effect is both subtle and dramatic at the same time. Years and years ago, it must be twenty-five at least, I visited Somerset Maugham's garden on the French Riviera. It was a breathtaking experience, one which I remember to this day, especially each time I work on a monochromatic bouquet. Maugham had landscaped the villa so that you walked through many separate gardens, each planted in flowers of a different color. There was a cool white one with tiny waterfalls, ferns, white cyclamen, white tulips—white everything. The blue garden was paved with lobelia, forget-me-nots, primroses, and delphiniums. And so it went. Past each border or beyond the next hedge, there was a new color to discover in all its many shades. Which reminds me, to approximate the airy effects of flowers in a garden, especially when making a monochrome arrangement, place the darker blossoms at the base of your bouquet and use lighter and lighter tints as you near the top. At the end of this chapter, you will find the most commonly used cut flowers listed by color. Consult this chart when you want to refresh your memory about the floral and chromatic possibilities within one color family. It is meant to be of equal value, whether you are shopping at a garden nursery or a florist shop.

The alternative to a monochromatic composition is, of course, composing a bouquet that utilizes several or all of the primary colors and their related shades. This is undoubtedly the most popular type of arrangement and contains few pitfalls. You may wish to mix different flowers in contrasting colors (red poppies, yellow tulips, blue bachelor buttons, and white baby's breath) or stick with the same flower in all its color possibilities (blue iris, yellow iris, orange iris, etc.). However, when combining primary colored flowers, avoid letting them fight it out for which one wins the viewer's attention. It is usually helpful to put white in such an arrangement as a sort of referee. As a matter of fact, the more white acts as a moderator between color families the more it emphasizes the good points of each. Where many use green ferns and leaves to accentuate areas of color, I find white frames with greater subtlety and blends all the floral members into a smoother whole. Don't let colored blossoms pop out of the arrangement and scream for attention until spots form before your eyes.

For me, there is nothing quite as special as an all-white bouquet. Like most women, I will always retain a memory of my first white childhood dress, the one with white embroidery on bodice and sleeves. That same brand-new, crispy light quality can be found in white on white floral arrangements. Luckily, there are so many possible flowers to work with when putting one together: delphin-

When You Mix Different Colors in One Bouquet

iums, hollyhocks, oleander, daffodils, narcissus, ranuculus, iris, snowballs, Japanese anemone, Shasta daisies, phlox, white violets (see plates 1 to 6). One year I had the very good fortune to plant a packet of seeds that produced an unusually large, solid white strain of sweet peas. Afraid that I might never come across the same stock again, I let the flowers bear their seeds and dried them for use the following season. This year's harvest of white sweet peas is the tenth generation of that self-perpetuation. A true, pure white-white is almost impossible to find in the garden. This may frustrate a perfectionist; but it allows flower arrangers to compose all-white bouquets with depth and texture, for white against nearly white truly shows up. Notice the greenish cast in a white zinnia, the slightly yellowish tint of oleander, the green at the base of sweet peas, and the pink that creeps into phlox. The variables when placed together produce a subtle, yet at the same time, striking bouquet. Or you can capitalize on the off-white tones in certain flowers to magnify and round out the color of another, using phlox with pink geraniums, and so on.

I am about to break the seemingly unwritten law that every book on flower arranging must have a color wheel included. They are an excellent aid in seeing how colors blend into each other and which ones are in contrast; but when it comes down to choosing the right flowers, in the right shades, for a particular setting, one needs more practical help. The following charts were drawn up to provide just that. You will notice that all of the commonly used cut flowers have been listed according to color, starting with the warm shades and ending with the cool ones. If you work only with flowers under one heading, the result will be a monochromatic bouquet; take ingredients from several columns and you will have a polychrome arrangement. These lists are lettered "A" through

"N." You will also find a chart that tells you which columns of flowers will produce Mixed Warm or Mixed Cool bouquets. Say you want to compose a rusty yellow arrangement to match a particular room setting. Simply go down the left-hand column until you reach "Rusty Yellow" and beside it will be "C + D + E + F"; meaning, that if you combine flowers from each of the so-lettered columns, the total arrangement will reflect the color you were after.

Two final points: While the Flower Color Charts start off with white, white is really not a color. Actually, it is all colors combined. And, being such, white has the chameleonlike ability to change its shade, depending upon what color it is near. Put a white rose next to a red Iceland poppy and it will become a warm white, but station the same rose close to green Bells of Ireland and it turns cool. The second principle you should always keep in mind is that certain dark shades, particularly purple, can fit into either the cool or the warm side of the color spectrum. Purple flowers mixed with red, pink, and magenta will produce a warm, purplish red bouquet. On the other hand, if you combine purple flowers with blues and violets, you will end up with a cool, purplish blue arrangement.

A FLOWER COLOR CHART

A. WARM WHITES
(Cream or yellow or pink tint)

anemone	nemesia
aster	pansy
baby's breath (dried)	phlox
candytuft (perennial)	primrose (English)
Christmas rose	ranunculus
chrysanthemum	rhododendron
cosmos	rose
daisy	scabiosa
English daisy	snapdragon
eremurus	snowball (fully opened)
feverfew	statice
foxglove	stocks
hare's-tail grass	sweet William
honesty	tulip
iris	wormwood
Japanese anemone	zinnia
magnolia	

B. COOL WHITES
(blue or green tint)

azalea	columbine
baby's breath (fresh)	cornflower
begonia	dahlia
bellflower	delphinium
camellia	fairy primrose
Canterbury bell	geranium
carnation	gladiolus
chrysanthemum	grape hyacinth

Iceland poppy

impatiens (Bizzy Lizzie)

iris

larkspur

lilac

lily (Madonna)

lily of the valley

narcissus (Paper Whites, Angel
   Tears, Thalia)

peach (flowering)

pears (flowering)

petunia

Queen Ann's lace

rose (Matterhorn, Piascali, Iceberg,
   Double De Coubert)

snowdrops

snowball (bud stage)

Spanish bluebell (Alba)

sweet pea

trillium

tulip

viola

wisteria

C. BRIGHT YELLOWS

acacia (mimosa)

black-eyed Susan

buttercup

calendula

California poppy

chrysanthemum

coreopsis

cosmos

daffodil

evening primrose

forsythia

gazania

geum

gloriosa daisy

Iceland poppy

marigold

narcissus

nasturtium

pansy

primrose (English)

ranunculus

rose (High Noon, Buccaneer)

sunflower

tulip

viola

zinnia

D. BUTTER, GOLD, AND ORANGE YELLOWS

autumn leaves

basket-of-gold

canna

carnation

chrysanthemum

cockscomb

columbine

cowslip

dahlia

daisy

dusty miller

freesia

gladiolus

goldenrod

hyacinth

iris

lily (Destiny, Joan Evans)

lupine (Russell)

painted daisy

petunia

phlox (annual)

pussywillow

rose (Eclipse, Lemon Spice, Lowell
Thomas)

slipperwort

snapdragon

sneezeweed

stocks

strawflower

wallflower

wheat (dry)

yarrow

zinnia

E. ORANGE

autumn leaves

calendula

California poppy

carnation

Chinese lantern

chrysanthemum

cosmos

dahlia

day lily

gaillardia

gladiolus

Iceland poppy

iris

lantana

lily (tiger, Japanese)

Maltese cross

marigold

nasturtium

nemesia

primrose (English, Japanese)

ranunculus

rose (Forty-Nine, Redgold,
Contempo)

snapdragon

sneezeweed

strawflower

tulip

viola

wallflower

zinnia

F. RUST, COPPER, AND BROWN TONES

autumn leaves

cattails

chrysanthemums (Rusty Joice,
Lilian Hock, Charm Spoon, Harry
James, Westfield Bronze,
Glenshades)

coreopsis (Dazzler)

day lily

dianthus ("Zebra," a border
carnation)

eremurus

freesia

gaillardia

gladiolus (Mokka, Toulouse-
Lautrec)

gloriosa daisy

iris (Bypsy Girl, Dutch Iris; Staten
Island, Mary Todd, Bearded Iris)

marigolds (Dainty Marietta, Rusty
Red, Redhead)

monkey flower

painted daisy

pansy (Roggli)

sneezeweed (Moehrheim Beauty,
Copper Spray)

strawflower

wallflower

zinnia, dwarf (Thumbelina)

G. ORANGE RED

carnation

chrysanthemum

cosmos

dahlia

geum

geranium

gladiolus

Iceland poppy

impatiens (Bizzy Lizzie)

nasturtium

nemesia

Oriental poppy

primrose (English)

pyrcantha (firethorn)

rose (Sarabande, single, Command
Performance, Simon Bolivar,
Tropicana)

ranunculus

salvia

snapdragon

sneezeweed

tithonia

tulip

verbena (Peruvian)

zinnia

A Bouquet of Colors ❧ 125

H. THE TRUE REDS

amaryllis

anemone

carnation

dahlia

Flanders poppy

geranium

gladiolus

Iceland poppy

ixia

Oriental poppy

pinks

rose (San Antonio,
   Gypsy, etc.)

tulip

zinnia

I. PINKS

aster

allium

amaryllis

begonia

Canterbury bells

carnation

chrysanthemum

clarkia

columbine

cornflower

cosmos

dahlia

geranium

gerbera

gladiolus

hollyhock

hyacinth

Iceland poppy

Japanese anemone

larkspur

lilly

lupine (Russell)

nemesia

nicotiana

Oriental poppy

painted daisy

peonies

petunia

phlox

pinks

primrose (English, fairy)

ranunculus

rose

scabiosa

shirley poppy

snapdragon

stock

strawflower

sweet pea

sweet Williams

tulip

umbrella plant

verbena

zinnia

J. MAGENTA AND ROSE REDS

aster	nicotiana
begonia	opium poppy
bleeding heart	painted daisy
carnation	peony
chrysanthemum	petunia
clarkia	phlox
cosmos	pinks
dahlia	primrose (English, fairy)
foxglove	ranunculus
freesia	rose
garden balsam	snapdragon
geranium	stock
gladiolus	sweet pea
godetia	sweet William
hollyhock	tulip
impatiens	verbena
lupine (Russell)	zinnia

K. TRUE BLUES

bachelor's button	Himalayan poppy
delphinium (Blue Jay, Blue Bird)	primrose (English)
forget-me-not (if grown in shade)	*scilla sibirica* (.bulb)
gentian	

L. VIOLET BLUES

ageratum	bellflower
allium	blue daisy (Felicia)
aster	Canterbury bells
baby blue-eyes	centaurea

Chinese peonies

clematis

columbine

crocus

delphinium

flax

gazania

gladiolus (Tintoretto)

grape hyacinth

hyacinth

hydrangea

iris (Dutch, Siberian, Spanish,
  Japanese, Bearded, etc.)

larkspur

nierembergia

pansy

petunia

phlox

primrose (English, fairy)

rose (Sterling Silver, Angel Face,
  Song of Paris)

saxifrage

scabiosa

Spanish bluebell

sweet pea

thistle

tulip (Maytime, Blue Parrot, The
  Bishop, Demster)

veronica

vinca

viola

violet

M. PURPLES

aster

campanula

Canterbury bells

columbine

cosmos

dahlia

delphinium

dianthus

freesia

gladiolus (Blue Conqueror)

iris

larkspur

lupine (Russell)

monkshood

pansy

Penstemon

petunia

sage

scabiosa

statice (sea lavender)

sweet pea

tradescantia

tulip (Black Tulip)

verbena (hybrids)

viola

violets

zinnia

N. GREENS

bells of Ireland

berries, in green stage

  (blackberry, etc.)

hopflowers

mignonette

hydrangea, pale green heads

Solomon's seal

vegetable leaves: celery,

  sorrel, horseradish,

  rhubarb, etc.

zinnia

MIXED WARM BOUQUET

mixed whites	A + B
yellowish white	A + B + C + D
mixed yellows	C + D
orange yellow	C + D + E
rusty yellow	C + D + E + F
rusty orange	E + F
rusty red	D + E + F + G
orange red	G + H
pinkish red	H + I
rose or magenta red	H + I + J
purplish red	H + I + J + M

MIXED COOL BOUQUET

mixed blues	K + L
purplish blue	K + L + M
greenish blue	K + L + N

❀ 9 ❀

The ABC's:
Acacia to Zinnia

For those of you who are gardeners interested in flower arranging, this chapter is devoted to the basic whens and hows of growing each of the flowers discussed in *Living with Flowers*. The lone exceptions are those plants that I do not grow but buy—statice, baby's breath, etc.—and the wild flowers, like mustard weed and lupine, which blanket the dry hillsides of southern California. Every region of the country has its own variety of the latter. They are free and go beautifully in informal arrangements.

Unless otherwise noted, all of the plants on the following chart require a neutral, rich, and loamy soil. *Neutral* refers to earth that is neither too alkaline nor overly acid. *Rich* is used when dirt has sufficient nitrogen (the greening element), phosphorous (governs the ultimate size of blossoms and the root system), and potash (for general vigor). *Loamy* denotes a light soil with good drainage. I have also indicated after the common name of each plant whether it is a perennial, an annual, or a biennial. Almost everyone knows that the first is planted just once and then comes up every year, but there is some confusion about the second and third terms.

Annuals, plants or bulbs, must be planted anew each annum and they will bloom later in the same year. *Biennials* must also be set in the ground each year; however, these will not flower until twelve months later.

It is wonderful that this vast country is so geographically and atmospherically varied, but it is hard on gardeners and botanists. Horticulturists all agree that, because of the infinite variables in sectional weather and temperature conditions (on our small piece of property, there is often a fifteen-degree variance between one area and another), it is impossible to make general rules about what will grow where and when. In the face of such professional warnings, it may have been foolhardy of me to prepare this East-West chart; but all of those easterners who visit California and ask, "But how do I grow them back home?" will understand why I tried.

For the purposes of this book, when I say "East," I have in mind those northern states, from the Great Lakes and Maine on down, that experience frost and heavy snowfalls. Naturally, those plants indigenous to the South, the West, or the North are in most cases not adaptable to other, inhospitable climatic regions. For example, bougainvillea is grown in California and Florida, but it will not survive in the cold, northern states unless raised in a greenhouse. Conversely, white lilacs need cold winters and will not blossom in California. But always remember that the majority of common flowers will grow on both coasts, it is just that their planting times are different. Most of the annuals and perennials that are planted in the spring in the East, for summer blooming, are planted in the West in the fall, for winter harvest. In the chart that follows, where a West Coast flower will not survive east of the Mississippi, the sad fact is so indicated with a plain no. If some plant might *just* make it, given optimum conditions, you will find a maybe under the East heading. *Greenhouse* means they must be raised in same and only taken out during the hot summer months.

Good luck, and remember that nature is full of incredible surprises.

CULTURE CHART

(Under the headings WEST *and* EAST *are listed the planting time,*

moisture needs, and light needs respectively for each plant)

	WEST	EAST
Acacia, perennial (*Acacia Baileyana*), this variety called "mimosa" on the East Coast	year around	greenhouse
	deep, infrequent waterings	same
	sun	same
Acacia, Gossamer Sydney (*Acacia longifolia floribunda*)	year around	greenhouse
	deep, infrequent waterings	same
	sun	same
Allium (*Tricuetrum*), one of the many flowering onion plants	bulbs in autumn	maybe
	frequent watering	same
	sun	same
Anemone, bulbous, annual (*Anemone coronaria*)	Oct. to Nov.	spring or autumn with heavy mulch
	average, beware of over-watering when dormant	same
	sun	same
Anemone, Japanese, perennial (*Anemone x. hybrida*)	autumn	early spring
	average	same
	full sun or partial shade	same
Artichoke, perennial (*Synara Scolymus*)	from containers in winter or early spring	no
	a great deal	
	sun	
Asparagus Fern, perennial (*Asparagus sprengeri*)	year round	good houseplant good hanging basket
	average	same
	partial or full shade	sun or partial shade

The ABC's: Acacia to Zinnia ❧ 133

	WEST	EAST
Aster, annual (*Callistephus chinensis*)	spring	same
	average	same
	full sun	same
Baby's Breath, annual (*Gypsophila paniculata*), NOTE: needs a slightly alkaline soil	best to seed in spring	midsummer, from cuttings
	average	same
	full sun or partial shade	full sun
Baby's Tears, perennial (*Soleirolia*)	anytime with moisture do not let it dry out	possible houseplant good in greenhouse
	a great deal	same
	full shade	partial shade
Bluebell of Scotland, perennial (*Campanula rotundifolia*)	anytime with moisture	spring or autumn
	needs moisture	same
	semi to full shade	sun to semishade
Cabbage, annual (*Brassica*)	fall and winter	early spring to midsummer
	lots of water	same
	sun and cool temperature	same
Camellia, perennial (*C. japonica*) NOTE: needs an acid soil	autumn	not many varieties are hardy; with care a good houseplant
	do not let dry out, but do not overwater	same
	shade to partial sun	same
Canterbury Bells, biennial (*Campanula medium*)	plant flats in Aug.–Sept. for next year	sow seed July–Aug., for bloom next year
	average	same
	sun to shade	sun to light shade
Carrot, annual (*Daucus carota sativa*)	anytime	after frost
	average	same
	sun, partial shade in summer	sun

	WEST	EAST
Celery (*Apium graveolens dulce*)	late summer, early fall; seeds	start with small plants after frost
	abundant	same
	sun to partial shade	sun
Chrysanthemum, Korean, perennial (*C. coreanum*)	put in plants, early spring	same
	water deeply	same
	sun to partial shade	sun
Chrysanthemum, pompon, perennial (*C. morifolium*)	same needs and care as above	
Cineraria, annual (*Senecio cruentus*)	autumn	from potted plants in spring
	water, but not wet feet	same
	shade	same
Columbine, biennial (*Aquilegia x. hybrida*)	autumn or early spring	in March, after frost
	on moist side	same
	partial shade to shade	partial shade
Corn, annual (*Zea mays*)	spring, when soil warm	after danger of frost
	deep watering	same
	sun	same
Cornflower, annual (*Centaurea Cyanus*)	early spring	after danger of frost
	average	same
	sun	same
Cosmos, annual (*Cosmos bipinnatus*)	sow seed, spring or summer	same
	drought resistant	same
	sun	same
Creeping Fig, perennial (*Ficus pumila*)	anytime	greenhouse, houseplant
	regular	same
	sun or shade	same

The ABC's: Acacia to Zinnia ❧ 135

	WEST	EAST
Cyclamen, perennial (*C. persicum*) NOTE: needs slightly acid soil	plants, June–Aug. for bloom in winter	best in greenhouse
	dry between waterings	same
	shade	same
Daffodil, perennial (*Narcissus pseudo-narcissus*)	late August to Nov.	same
	average	same
	full sun to light shade	same
Daisy, African (*Gerbera x. jamesonii*)	late summer, early fall	greenhouse, set in garden in summer
	cannot withstand drought	regular
	sun, partial shade in hot areas	sun
Daisy, Gloriosa, perennial, treated as annual on West Coast (*Rudbeckia hirta*); a hybridized black-eyed Susan	spring-early summer	sow seeds Feb.–March
	adequate	same
	sun	same
Daisy, Ox-eye, perennial (*Chrysanthemum leucanthemum vulgaris*); also called the European Daisy	spring	same
	average	same
	sun	same
Daisy, Shasta, perennial (*Chrysanthemum maximum*)	spring	same
	likes water	same
	sun to partial shade	same
Delphinium, perennial (*D. aconitum*)	sow in July–Aug. (flats); set out young plants, Oct.	sow March–April; transplant, June–July
	regular watering	same
	sun to partial shade	full sun
Digitalis (Foxglove), biennial (*Digitalis purpurea*)	seed in August	plants in May
	average	same
	filtered sun	same

	WEST	EAST
Eucalyptus (Tasmanian Blue Gum), perennial (*E. globulus*)	anytime little, drought resistant full sun, shade, anything	no
Fern, Leather, perennial (*Rumohra adiantifelium*)	anytime generous and regular partial or full shade	greenhouse, possible houseplant same same
Feverfew, annual (*Chrysanthemum parthenium*), so hardy often considered a weed—this is the cultivated variety with yellow leaves	sow seeds in spring average sun and light shade	same same full sun
Firethorn, perennial (*Pyracantha coccinea*) NOTE: may be deciduous in colder northern regions	anytime average sun to partial shade	spring same full sun
Forget-me-not, Chinese, annual (*Cynoglossum amabile*)	seed, fall or spring average shade	seed early to bloom first year same sun
Frais-de-bois, perennial (*Fragraria vesca*)	fall a good deal woodsy shade	June to fall same same
Freesia, perennial (*Freesia armstrongii*)	bulbs in fall average sun to partial shade	bulbs indoors in pots, Oct. to Jan. same sun
Fuchsia, perennial (*Fuchsia hybrida*)	early spring	only in summer outdoors, carry through winter indoors

	WEST	EAST
Fuchsia, perennial (*Fuchsia hybrida*)	lots of watering and misting	same
	filtered sun to shade	same
Geraniums, perennial (*Pelargonium hortorum*)	anytime	houseplant or summer bedding after frost
	keep on dry side	same
	sun, shade in very hot areas	sun
Iris (bulbous), perennial (*I. xiphioides*)	Aug. to Oct.	same
	regular but little water during summer dormancy	same
	sun to partial shade	sun
Iris (rhizomatous), perennial (*I. germanica*)	July to Aug.	same
	ample	same
	sun to partial shade	full sun
Ivy, Algerian, perennial (*Hedera canariensis*)	early spring	not hardy outdoors; use as houseplant
	water well in hot periods	water regularly to keep from drying out
	sun or shade	same
Ivy, English, perennial (*Hedera helix*)	spring on	spring
	water well in hot periods	same
	shade	same
Jerusalem Cherry, perennial (*Solanum Pseudocapsicum*)	anytime, from ripe cherries	only as pot plant, inside in winter, outside in summer.
	lots of water	same
	shade	some sun
Kalanchoe ("Brilliant Star"), perennial (*Kalanchoe blossfeldiana*)	anytime	a houseplant
	dry between waterings	same
	sun	same

	WEST	EAST
Lemon, perennial (*Citrus limon*)	any, but best in spring	houseplant except in Florida
	on dry side, with occasional deep waterings	same
	sun	sun
Lettuce (head), annual (*Lactuca sativa*)	from end of summer to next heat spell	early spring; start seeds 6–8 weeks before outdoor planting
	constant moisture	same
	partial shade	sun
Lettuce (romaine), annual (*Lactuca sativa*)	same culture as head lettuce but more tolerant to heat; hence better for summer growing	
Lily, Goldband, perennial (*Lilium auratum*) NOTE: keep tops in sun, roots in shade	early spring	spring or autumn
	ample, throughout year	same
	sun	same
Lily, Regal, perennial (*Lilium regale*)	spring or fall	autumn or spring
	ample throughout year	same
	head in sun, roots shaded	same
Lily, Rubrum, perennial (*Lilium speciosum*)	fall or spring	same
	ample throughout year	same
	partial shade; keep soil cool; tolerates some shade.	same
Lily-of-the-Nile, perennial (*Agapanthus Africanus*)	plant in ground, anytime	set pots into garden in summer
	average	same
	sun to partial shade	sun
Lime, perennial (*Citrus aurantifolia*)	best in early spring	only as houseplant, except Florida
	water deeply every other week for established trees	in hot weather, those in containers may need daily watering

	WEST	EAST
Lime, perennial (*Citrus aurantifolia*)	sun	bright light when container indoors
Lobelia, annual (*L. erinus*)	when weather is cool	start seeds indoors, Feb. to March
	heavy	same
	partial shade	sun
Marguerite, perennial (*Chrysanthemum frutescens*)	spring	same, but grows as annual
	regular	same
	partial shade	sun
Marigolds, African, annual (*Tagetes Erecta*)	spring	same
	average, but will survive with little water	same
	full sun	same
Marigolds, French, annual (*Tagetes patula*)	culture same as above	
Marigold, Pot, annual (*Calendula officinalis*), as an herb, flower petals used to give color to stews, puddings	sow seeds in late summer for winter-spring bloom	sow seeds in April; set plants in May
	average if drainage good	same
	sun	same
Morning Glory, annual (*Ipomoea purpurea*)	May; will bloom earlier if seeds started indoors in March	same
	water moderately	same
	sun	same
Moss, Scotch, perennial (*Sagina subulatu*) NOTE: Irish moss is greener but has same growing conditions	spring to autumn	same
	water generously	same
	shade	semi-shade
Narcissus, perennial (*Narciseus peotaz*)	Nov. or when soil is cool	Aug. to Nov.
	water well when planted, then only in hot	same

	WEST	EAST
Narcissus, perennial (Narciseus peotaz)	weather; start normal watering when foliage is up	
	light shade to shade	full sun to light shade
Nasturtium, annual (*Trapaeolum majus*) NOTE: along with Marigolds, Zinnia, and Tithonia, these are *very easy* flowers to grow from seed	early spring	same
	average	same
	sun or partial shade	full sun
Nightshade, Paraguayan, perennial (*Solanum rantonetti*)	whenever	never
	average	no
	sun to partial shade	no
Oleander (single), perennial (*Nerium oleander*), there are "petite" varieties, three to four feet tall	anytime	grow in pots, move inside with first frost
	little	same
	sun	same
Orange, perennial (*Citrus sinensis*)	best in early spring	only as houseplant except in Florida; take out in summer
	water deeply every other week; don't overdo it if soil drains poorly	trees in containers, in sun, may need watering every day
	sun	as much light as possible
Oxalis, Yellow, perennial (*Oxalis pes-caprae*)	fall	potted plants; keep indoors in winter
	average	same
	sun or shade	sun
Pansy, perennial treated as an annual (*Viola tricolor hortensis*)	plants in fall; seeds, mid-July to mid-August	sow seeds indoors, Jan. to Feb.; plant in ground early spring
	regular	same
	sun to partial shade; keep cool	sun

The ABC's: Acacia to Zinnia ❧ 141

	WEST	EAST
Parsnip, annual (*Pastinaca sativa*)	fall	early spring
	average	same
	sun or shade	sun
Peppermint, perennial (*Mentha pipereta*)	spring	same
	likes moist soil	same
	partial shade	same
Periwinkle, Madagascar, annual (*Catharanthus rosea*)	spring	spring
	likes moisture	same
	sun to partial shade	same
Petunia, annual (*Petunia x hybrida*)	early spring from seeds	sow seeds indoors, plant outside after end of frost
	moderate, hybrids sensitive to overwatering	same
	sun to partial shade	sun
Phalaenopsis (Moth orchid), perennial NOTE: lives off air in soil; plant in redwood chips	a greenhouse plant or under ideal house conditions	same
	requires humidity, mist daily, water once a week	same
	enough for warmth, 60–70° at night, 70–85° in daytime	same
Phlox, annual (*Phlox drummondii*)	fall	spring
	adequate	same
	sun to partial shade	sun
Pine, Norfolk Island, perennial (*Araucaria excelsa*)	anytime	good houseplant
	abundant	semidry between waterings
	sun to partial shade	bright light, full sun not required
Pinks (red border carnation), perennial (*Dianthus plumavius*)	winter to early spring	best from plants, in spring
	avoid overwatering	average

	WEST	EAST
Pinks (red border carnation), perennial (*Dianthus plumavius*)	full sun, light shade in hot areas	full sun
Poppy, California, perennial (*Eschscholzia Californica*)	sow seeds in fall	sow Sept. or March
	drought tolerant but the more water it gets the fuller and taller the plant	same
	full sun	same
Poppy, Iceland, annual (*Papaver nudicaule*)	fall	early spring
	average	same
	sun	same
Primrose, English, perennial (*Primula polyanthus*) NOTE: requires a light acid soil	fall	early spring, early fall
	generous	same
	partial or full shade	partial shade
Primrose, fairy, annual (*Primula malacoides*)	From flats, Oct.–Nov.	sow in early summer for fall bloom
	plenty of water	same
	light shade; best kept cool	sun to light shade
Queen Ann's Lace (wild carrot), annual (*Davcus carota*)	anytime	spring
	average	average
	sun and partial shade	sun
Radish, annual (*Raphanus sativus*)	anytime, except in hot weather	anytime after frost
	ample, to keep in active growth	same
	sun or partial shade	sun
Rose, perennial (*Rosa*) NOTE: the breeds of roses I raise are: Yellow–High Noon and Buccanneer, both grandiflora; Orange Red—Gypsy (hybrid tea), Sarabande (hybrid	winter, early spring for bare root stock; from containers, anytime	same
	loves water but not wet feet	same
	sun	same

tea) and Montazuma (grandiflora); Pink —Charlotte Armstrong (hybrid tea); White— Pascali (hybrid tea); Deep Red—Chrysler Imperial (hybrid tea); Orange plus Red bicolor—Joseph's Coat (climber) and Forty-nine (hybrid tea); Silver Lavender—Sterling Silver (hybrid tea); and I would cultivate all of the old-fashioned single and cabbage roses if I could find them

	WEST	EAST
Ranunculus, perennial (*Ranunculus asiaticus*)	plant tubers in Nov.	after frost, lift tubers before frost
	water after planting, not again till growth starts	same
	sun, cool climate	same
Snowball, perennial (*Viburnum*)	anytime	spring or autumn
	generous	same
	sun or partial shade	same
Sorrel, perennial (*Rumex acetosa*)	anytime but hot weather	spring
	generous	same
	sun to partial shade	sun
Spider Plant, perennial (*Chlorophytum comosum variegatum*)	spring-summer; can grow in ground	houseplant
	likes moisture but do not overwater	same
	shade	same
Squash (summer, yellow, acorn), annual (*Cucurbita*)	late spring	same
	generous	same
	full sun; love heat	same

	WEST	EAST
Strawberry, perennial	late summer, fall	early spring
	do not let plants dry out	same
	sun	same
Sunflower, annual (*Helianthus annuus*)	spring	same
	very little	same
	full sun	same
Sunflower, Mexican, annual (*Tithonia*)	from seeds in spring	start seeds indoors in March; set in ground after frost
	very little, drought resistant	same
	full sun	same
Sweet Alyssum, annual (*Lobularia maritima*)	anytime	spring; seeds or from plants
	average	same
	sun to light shade	sun
Sweet Pea, annual (*Lathyrus odoratus*)	Aug. to early Sept.	as soon as ground can be worked
	generous	same
	sun plus shade	sun
Tickseed, annual (*Coreopsis verticillata*)	spring	seeds early spring; plants, spring or fall
	drought resistant	same
	full sun	same
Tomato, annual (*Lycopersicum esculentum*)	put in plants April to June	when frost danger is past
	frequent deep watering at first, less often once established	same
	sun	same
Tulip, perennial (*Tulipa*)	store in refrigerator 6–8 weeks before planting from Nov. to Jan.	Oct. or when weather cools

	WEST	EAST
Tulip, perennial (*Tulipa*)	needs water when growing but only in winter when very dry	same
	sun	same
Turnip, annual (*Brassica rapa*)	Sept.–March	April, then again in July or August
	average	same
	sun	same
Verbena, perennial (*Peruviana x hybrida*)	spring	no; instead, use the *annual* verbena x hybrida; it is multicolored
	less frequent but deep waterings	same
	sun and heat	same
Viola (Paris strain), perennial (*Viola pedata*)	(has same needs and growing habits as pansy)	
Wisteria, perennial (*W. sinensis*)	when dormant; winter to early spring	same
	ample when in bloom or growth	same
	sun to partial shade in hot areas	sun
Zinnia, annual (*Zinnia elegans*)	spring-early summer	after last frost
	average	same
	full sun	same

❦ 10 ❦

A Blooming Life

I have a warm place in my heart for the Flower Children of the sixties. They may have lost some causes and some friends but that idealistic rabble poked a few refreshing holes in our traditional thinking, among them, the concept that nature was a richer provider than General Motors. It is not sheer coincidence that Americans started "thinking green" in those years and that today, in the eighties, a house without flowers, in one form or another, is not a home.

While bowls and pitchers of blooms are certainly the most accepted approach to bringing inside the beauty and joy of the outdoors, they are not the only way to color one's life with flowers. I am not suggesting that women get tangled up in daisy chains or that men should go back to wearing boutonnieres, although it is not a bad idea, but there are dozens of little things that can be done around the house to spread the joy. They need not be big productions or expensive ones. Here are some of these incidental ways to keep your life in bloom, year-round.

For years, I have been decorating butter crocks and dishes with flowers. When I lived in New York City, the easiest flowers to get for such a garnish were daisies and pansies; but with a garden of my own, it made sense to use an edible blossom such as nasturtium. When using nasturtium, take the petals off a perfect blossom and then reassemble the blossom on top of the butter. After gently pressing the petals into place, add a few peppercorns to simulate the heart of the flower. When nasturtium are not in season, attractive designs can be made using sprigs of watercress and parsley, or you may want to cut petal shapes from the skin of a radish and arrange them in the form of a stylized bloom. Nasturtiums have a wonderful, tangy flavor and look marvelous sprinkled over a green salad. When squash are in season, I add their blossoms to the bowl, also. In such salads, be sure to use a very light dressing so that the flowers can be fully savored.

I often go several steps further in using vegetables as substitutes for flowers and make an entire bouquet carved from our produce garden. I use turnips, carrots, radishes, squash and tomato rinds, and mushrooms for the mock blossoms, while spinach, bib lettuce, carrot tops, parsley, radish, and squash blossoms serve as the green filler. It makes a lovely spring or summer centerpiece and is really simpler to fashion than one might imagine. To create the bouquet, outline the flower shapes with a soft lead pencil on stiff slices of turnip, and then cut them out with a pointed knife and a very sharp scissors. Then build up the face of each blossom with strips, slivers, and rosettes carved out of the other vegetables and stick each on a piece of florist wire to serve as the stem. To preserve crispness, keep the floral parts in ice water while you do the assembling, then spray with water and store the finished bouquet in the refrigerator until just before show time.

In the same way, one can raid the vegetable garden—or the

supermarket produce section—for candle holders to use at informal parties. It does not take more than a few minutes to scoop out a candle hole from the bulbous bases of crookneck, acorn, and summer squash, red onion and scored radishes, regular and Chinese cabbage, artichoke and mushroom. With the exception of the squashes and artichoke these creations will not last for very long. However, that is just as well, for they are conceived as an amusing aside and I would not want to live with the joke day in and day out. The arrangement of vegetable flowers and some of these candlesticks is a fine combination on a family Thanksgiving table or at a children's party, not to mention a birthday party for the calorie-conscious.

Thanksgiving is an extra wonderful day for gardeners and flower lovers. We have a whole year of daily miracles and gifts to be grateful for. Last year, we invited four close friends to share our blessings. I was glad there were not more, for that would have meant eating in the dining room rather than in the kitchen, and a harvest meal should be celebrated amidst the sounds and sights and smells of the cooking feast. There was no room on the laden table for a full-size, legitimate floral centerpiece, so all around the kitchen and in the corner of the banquette on which some guests sat, I placed hollowed-out pumpkins—plastic containers were hidden within—filled with the yellow and orange colors of fall, mixing live flowers with dried grasses and seed pods. To make up for the absence of flowers on the table itself, the linen was embroidered with blossoms, there was a large display of edible raw vegetables, and scooped-out gourds held the "musts" of Thanksgiving: cranberries, nuts, fresh fruits, and so on. For dessert there was a chestnut puree topped with whipped cream topped with white violets.

A Garden of Candle Holders

PLATE 30

Flowers for Thanksgiving

PLATE 45

There is no denying that one has to work a little harder to achieve a Christmas atmosphere in sunny southern California. I try to spread decorative reminders of the season throughout the house, rather than just concentrating on the one room where the Christmas tree stands. As a matter of fact, we do not have one big tree but six or eight small ones. Each is kept alive from one year to the next in a pot or tub stationed in a cool spot on the terrace. None is so large that, once decorated, it cannot stand on a table as a living Christmas bouquet, and we station two in the bedroom, several in the kitchen, one in the study, and the others, usually the biggest ones, brighten the living room.

For some time, I have been training yellow and white miniature mum bushes into large crowned trees, standing four feet high. These two are brought indoors for the holidays. They are the same kind that sell in florist shops for anywhere from $25 to $40, so if you are lucky enough to be given one as a present try to nurse it through to the following year. When the mum blossoms are finished, put the tree outside—in cold climates, they would have to sit through the winter in a greenhouse—cutting back the crown but maintaining its bushy shape. About four months before it comes into bloom again, start an every-other-week fertilizing program. As the plant begins to throw off new green shoots, snip back those which do not conform to the desired profile and be sure to take off all suckers and stem buds from the trunk of the small tree.

Just before Christmas, the lower branches of our fir trees are pruned. This, of course, makes them grow taller and fills out their tops, but it also provides a good supply of pine boughs for Christmas decorations. I do the same thing with branches from the silver eucalyptus and mix them with sprays of holly and cuttings from berry bushes, often adding a few flowers to the arrangement. This is a very inexpensive and simple way to dress up a display of greens and fall leaves brought back from a drive in the country. The brighter the blossoms the better. Incidentally, one can use these same commonly found ingredients to make a Christmas wreath. All that is needed is a shallow, round basket. Cut a hole in the center and around the opening build up circular layers of branches, leaves, and berries, securing them to the wicker bottom with florist wire. Also, tie on unshelled nuts, pine cones, or whatever you wish, being sure to cover the concentric lips of the basket with foliage. The completed basket can be used as is for a table centerpiece or hung upright as a wreath.

Among last year's indoor trees, one was fashioned from a small star pine, also known as Norfolk Island pine and available in most nurseries and flower shops. I preferred it (plate 46) to the others because, without having used a single traditional decoration, just a strand of tiny lights and daffodils, it conveyed to me the real meaning of Christmas. Constructing this daffodil and fir display took less than half an hour. With so many other things that must be done at Christmas, it is wise not to make a big, time-consuming production of every holiday arrangement.

Christmas
Table Settings

It has been a few years since my husband got up at dawn to see what Santa Claus left by the tree, so he heartily endorses the European custom of exchanging gifts and having Christmas supper on the night of the 24th. I love the warm peace of that candlelit meal, the memories it stirs of times past and the quiet talk of hopes to come. Perhaps that is why my flower arrangements and table setting on Christmas Eve are quite traditional. The table seems a bit crowded at first, but the jam-up breaks before we sit down. Four miniature Christmas trees—a genus of spruce used for making bonsai, decorated with Mylar cutouts and single strands of metallic knitting yarn—are presents for our guests and we place these on the sideboard when we sit down to dine.

Once the leisurely supper is over, we go to the freezer and bring out a bottle of Aquavit encased in a flower-filled block of ice and we will toast each other one last time. It is a very festive way of serving any 100-proof (a lesser alcohol content will freeze) liquor that requires chilling: Russian vodka, pear brandy, and the like. To do it yourself, place the bottle in a one-pound coffee tin. Select the flowers—for our holiday season, they are holly, white daisies, and maidenhair fern—and wedge them down between the bottle and the inside of the can. Use one rather stiff floral element, such as the holly, to keep all the flowers from floating to the top when you fill with water, which is the last step. Place the container in the freezer section of your refrigerator. Before serving, run hot water over the sides of the can until the blooming iceberg slips free.

Naturally, the flowers embedded in the ice should be changed according to the occasion. For a recent summer outdoor luncheon, pansies, white geraniums, and nasturtiums were used.

Easter, of course, means spring, the beginning of a fresh new year for flower lovers. The temptation is to celebrate the occasion with big and bold bouquets. I like to go the other way, remembering that it is a gentle season; hence, the table arrangements stress simplicity. The bouquets are low-lying affairs. I do not want a "conversation piece" to interfere with conversation. For most of us, doilies went out with the demise of the day laundress; which is just as well, since there was something very fusty and dusty about them. Nevertheless, there are times when you want to soften a broad expanse of cold china. To do so on the Easter service plates, I made a wreath of ivy leaves and daisy blossoms. Had I not used a tablecloth that day, each of the bouquets in the twig bird's nests —really French wine bottle coasters—would have been encircled

Decorating an

Easter Table

in a similar fashion. The flower and leaf design is kept from falling apart by toothpicks.

You have seen that there is not one papier-mâché turkey, snow-sprayed Santa Claus, haloed angel, or chocolate bunny rabbit in my holiday floral arrangements. I do not want to "bah, humbug" these symbolic creatures. I simply have no great desire to share my table with a bunch of stuffed dolls. Flowers are flowers, toys are toys. One should use the former to capture the spirit of a day without resorting to props.

Flowers for Other Holidays

This past year, I tested the axiom about good marriages being partially built upon a mutual sense of humor. On Valentine's Day my husband sat down at the breakfast table to discover a cactus-shaped heart I had found growing in the dunes, with one red rose stuck on a thorn. The Fourth of July bouquet is hardly a joke, but I

do find it great fun. Red geraniums and just the blossoms from white and blue delphiniums were tucked into a multisectioned, pyramid container. Delphiniums, sad to say, do not last for very long as a cut flower. Fortunately, though, they bloom and wither from the bottom up; so, when lower flowers are falling off, the upper buds may just be opening. The Fourth of July arrangement is one example of how you may take advantage of this inverse progression and use the flower to its very end.

While the current vogue for dried flowers is understandable, and I do use them occasionally myself, I must confess they leave me cold. No matter how perfectly they are treated in silica or the other drying agents, there is always something missing, and that something is *life*. The colors retained are marvelously accurate, but there is an ever so slight tint of grey, the pallor of death. Besides, the beauty and excitement in a flower is dependent on more than just color and smell. There must be texture, the trapper and reflector of light. Dehydration mummifies that quality. For me, one of the principal delights of working with fresh flowers is that there is always something new and different to look forward to. Like vegetables, it is fine to have dried beans once in a while, but how one awaits the sensation of garden-fresh green beans. Change is the spice of a visual life. When my garden is resting, I often buy huge bundles of fresh statice and let them dry in large baskets around the house. They will last for about two months before accumulating a pound of dust and the flowers begin to fall. Interestingly, I feel no pang when throwing them away as I do with live flowers, no matter how wilted the latter have become.

With all this anti-dried flower talk, I must admit a passion for baby's breath. However, I am not completely untrue to my colors for I buy it *fresh* and by the armful from a commercial geranium

Pros and Cons of Dried Flowers

grower who also has a sideline in statice. At the height of the dried flower craze, the Japanese owner told me, apologetically, "It's those dead flowers, Ms. Hargarsaki, who help me keep the geraniums alive." And I, in turn, depend upon the gossamer baby's breath to gently round out a floral grouping, or best of all, I'll place a cloud of them in a pitcher, all by themselves. Then there are certain holders, like a three-tier wire basket hanging in our bedroom which would be in serious trouble were it filled with anything but dried flowers.

Epilogue

As with a garden, people's lives change over the years. However and this is where we become the true guardians of Nature, whether the transformation is for better or worse is up to Man, the planter and planner, the one blessed with intelligence and hope.

Between the time the manuscript of *Living with Flowers* was sent to the publisher and now, as I sit checking the final proofs, we moved twenty-five miles further west. Literally, as far as we could go, for our new home is at the edge of a bluff overlooking the Pacific Ocean. It is a tiny place, about a quarter the size of the former dwelling and the total gardening area consists of an 800-square-foot terrace. Friends and family all bemoaned our selling and asked, "How can you leave such a paradise?" They, of course, were not responsible for the upkeep of the acre and a half. But after nearly two decades, it was not easy. The morning the moving vans pulled out of the driveway, I walked through the garden of old friends for the last time. Stopping to fix first this flower, then that one, tears mixed with the dew on their petals.

However, one of those departing trucks contained my favorite hanging baskets, patio tubs, and portable bouquets. We pulled up flagstone slabs from the oceanside terrace, making room for small flower, salad, and vegetable beds. At this moment, looking out through the living-room windows toward the endless expanse of blue sea, my vista includes a foreground of potted white marguerities and oleanders, white rose trees, and begonias. High and low containers hold yellow petite marigolds mixed with white alyssum. Hanging baskets form a see-through curtain of white impatients, white cascade petunias, fuchsia, and lobelia. Last night we ate a just-picked salad of *arugula*, Bibb lettuce, and red-ripe tomatoes.

People and flowers can be transplanted to smaller living space and still flourish. In fact, they are often happier that way. I know we are.

Index